Canadian Historical Mysteries Collection

Rum Bullets and Cod Fish - Nova Scotia

Sleuthing the Klondike – Yukon

Who Buried Sarah- New Brunswick

The Flying Dutchman – British Columbia

Bad Omen - Nunavut

Spectral Evidence – Newfoundland

The Seance Murders – Saskatchewan

The Canoe Brigade – Quebec

Discarded – Manitoba

Twice Hung - Prince Edward Island

The Tom Tompson Mystery – Ontario

A Killer Whisky – Alberta

Spectral Evidence

Canadian Historical Mysteries - Newfoundland

Eileen Charbonneau and Jude Pittman

Print ISBNs
Amazon print 9780228629481
Ingram Spark 9780228629498
BWL Print 9780228629504

BWL Publishing Inc.

Books we love to write ...
Authors around the world.

http://bwlpublishing.ca

Acknowledgements

BWL Publishing acknowledges the Government of Canada and the Canada Book Fund for its financial support in creating the Canadian Historical Mysteries collection.

BWL Publishing acknowledges the Province of Alberta for their ongoing support through the Alberta Publisher's Cultural Industry Operating Grant.

Table of Contents

Chapter 1
Home from the Sea

The first name given to me by my mother, *Rising from the Wave* came because I was born in *Lampok*, the water world's swell, on board my father's ship. He insists the gale becalmed to hear my coos and suckling sounds. He sometimes calls me *ma petite onde*, his little wave. I'm a good person to have around in a storm still, he says.

But I am also deeply rooted here, on the island my father's people call Newfoundland. They came from across the wide Atlantic in ships with great white wings. My mother's peoples, the Mi'kmaq and the Beothuk, who call me many variations of my first name, were watching from shore. They were not surprised by the new people's arrival. Long ago a holy woman had a vision of islands of trees floating towards us, So, we greeted the tall ships with joy, eager to trade. We even added their spirit world of Christianity within our own.

My father sought refuge here, away from wars and kings. Newfoundland is a good place, full of the bounties of earth and sea and sky. But the wars followed.

We were in one of those wars in that Spring of 1692 as I scanned the horizon on a cold and fog laced spring day before dawn. My companions on our cliffs above St. John's, were gulls, our colorful sea parrots, and rough-legged hawks. And soon came the sound of Randall Kelly's step assisted by a walking stick.

"You are up before the sun," I said quietly.

A gusting, like the one our island ponies make through their noses, came out of him. "I tread toes first in the moccasins you made for me, Charlotte Jaddore," he complained, loud enough to turn the head of a curious gull.

I turned. "Aye, but you took a winding way, giving me more time to hear your approach."

Randall Kelly grinned. "Straight paths make for dull stories. I hope you have reaped some stories for me over the winter with your grandmothers."

"I have. How did you know I was returned from the inland?"

"The dust has been flying out your windows."

"Ah. Spring cleaning."

"And the praise of your hired helper, after you noticed her hurting arm and took to your concoctions for help. What kind of a crier would I be to not know the comings and goings of St. John's and all of Avalon beyond? You cut me to the very quick, lady!"

My smile ran away from me as we sat together on a nearby outcrop of rock. I miss our past together when Randall called me "child" and "sprite." The "lady" had begun after my return last year. It honors me and my growing into my womanhood, but it feels strange still.

I have known Randall Kelly since I was not much more than a toddling child and he an orphaned immigrant of ten years. Because of the injury he suffered over his Atlantic crossing, he was judged unfit for his indenture-contracted seaman's duties. But he was more than fit to nurse my family through the smallpox that descended soon after, killing my mother and her babe, driving my father near madness in his grief. We all bear the marks of that terrible time. Randall Kelly bears them the lightest, showing us the way, for he had already survived the loss of his own family in a place called Waterford, Ireland.

My father bought out the terms of Randall's indenture. In the years that followed, others saw him as our lame servant, doing the work of women, the cooking and cleaning and household management. But he became my brother as he sat beside me at my lessons. We gained our love of books and knowledge together. Soon, we'd formed a new family—Randall, my father, and I. His literacy, combined with his sanguine humor and curiosity made it natural for our small community of St. John's to offer him the brass bell of Town Crier.

Randall had his own rooms now, in an old storage barn he acquired because it had a window that faced north. He carved more windows in that wall so that he could get that beautiful artist's light, even on our many cloudy days. When my father brought paintings from Amsterdam to our shores, Randall was in their thrall. The portraits and landscapes became his teachers as his drawings acquired color and skill. His barn is his home now, and he sleeps below its rafters.

The sign above our tavern-the Sea Parrot- bears Randall's portrait of the nesting birds that live on our cliffs. Those seeking to decorate their dwellings with more than fishing tackle and clothes hooks are happy to keep our artist fed and clothed in exchange for the products of his craft.

Randall leaned his dear face against the leaping dolphin he'd carved into his walking stick. He looked at me with his artist's eye now, as if judging how well I fit into his mind's new composition, along with land and sea, shrouded in morning fog. Suddenly, his brow quirked up, the way it used to when he suspected me of keeping a secret. "Are all shelves and storerooms made ready for this year's new goods?"

"They are."

"Aye, then. And now, Charlotte Jaddore, with your powers beyond mere mortal ken, might ye know when the winds will blow the *Esperance* in?"

"Do not you tread over that territory with me," I admonished him. "George Wyatt already thinks I have dried up his cow."

"Does he? And have you?"

"Pish. What do I want with her calf's food? You are a strange people who steal eggs from the birds and milk meant for the young of others."

He laughed. "Now you sound like your grandmothers. How did those fine women fare over the winter?"

"They are well. Their message for you is to study the weasel over our coming crowded months."

Randall Kelly is one of the few my grandmothers have allowed close to the inland camps of the Beothuk and Mi'kmaq. He is a smallpox survivor. That is part of the reason they feel safe. The other lies inside our artist crier himself, who both my grandmothers consider a holy person. *Holds Two Spirits* is their Medicine name for him. They send me back to St. John's every spring with another animal for Randall Kelly to study, to gather around him, to give him strength and protection.

Randall's laughing eyes, the color of seagrass in summer now stilled. "Tell the grandmothers that I will risk the weasel people's bites of displeasure to follow their advice." He looked at his hands then. "And thank them for me, will ye?"

"Of course," I agreed.

"It's glad I am that they see me as a scholar studying the world around."

We had achieved twenty-five and seventeen years of life on Mother Earth, Randall and I. But I suspect we both missed our free childhoods, before I ran my father's house and business. Before Randall took up his paints and the crier's bell, back when we were welcomed like unruly puppies into all the communities of Avalon—the English and Dutch of St. John's, the French at Plaisance, and the Irish dory fishermen of our many bays and coves. We were welcomed even into the high valleys of the mountains and barrens, where our trading partners, the Mi'kmaq and the reclusive earlier people of my great-grandmother, the Beothuk, abide.

The east wind picked up suddenly, blowing away the night's fog. Randall reached into his pouch for his spyglass. He scanned the horizon, past the harbor bay, just as the sun was appearing over the eastern edge of the world the Mi'kmaq call Turtle Island.

"I knew it! I knew trudging up here after you would bear fruit!"

He handed me the glass, took up the shell horn that he used for long-distance summoning of the town's attention, and blew. I stood beside my friend, letting my blue apron fly like a flag of welcome. For out there, among the last of the icebergs, was a ship we both knew well. The *Esperance.* My father was home from the sea.

The gathered people at the dock parted upon my approach. I lifted my skirts and ran to the *Esperance* as the gangplank was set in place. Every mother's child of them knew they would not get a first look at the wines, the lemons and oranges, the stockings, and French silks. Not until my father had given his heir and business partner a proper greeting. His arms, his salt tang smell mixed with clove, the quill and bead decoration that dangled from his ear- all were home to me. My world was not returned in balance until his quartermaster began a reel on his pipe and we'd danced a swinging circle in each other's arms.

As the tune finished, we heard Randall Kelly's bell, then his powerful voice.

"Hear ye! Hear ye! Be it known that by the grace of Divine Providence and the skill of her officers and crew, the good ship fashioned of fleet Bermuda cedar known as the Esperance, in their Majesties King William and Queen Anne's port of St. John's in the Colony of Avalon, has landed this eleventh day of April in the year of our Lord sixteen hundred and ninety-two! As first of the season into port, Martin Jaddore is hereby declared Fleet Captain and Fishing Admiral! Is this not a day to bring our poor wintering souls joy? A day altogether calling

to mind the words of our own gracious late
and lamented governor poet?

'*The air in Newfoundland is wholesome
good,*

The fire as sweet as any made of wood,

*The water, very rich, both salt and
fresh,*

*The earth more rich, you know it is no
less*

*Where all are good, fire, water, earth
and air,*

*What man made of these four would not
live there?*'"

Loud cheering followed his recitation of
Robert Hayman's verse. Amid the jubilation,
my father growled before he whispered in
my ear, "Poetry? More like royal sanctioned
versifying lies out of that Devonshire pirate!
Did we not have Randall Kelly recite enough
Shakespeare in his youth to know the
difference?"

* * *

My father's approval of the ship-shape
condition of our storerooms' shelves and
bins made all the tedious clearing of
grandmother spider's winter weavings
worthwhile. Soon the *Esperance*'s crewmen
filled them with the goods to be traded for
our salted cod in the fishing season ahead. I
welcomed the wobbly-kneed fishermen,
those who returned each year to the shores

16

of St. John's. I asked about their families and exploits over the winter. I greeted the newcomers among them, each in his own language, be it French, Spanish, Portuguese or Dutch. It seldom failed to bring a smile or ease the fear in their eyes.

Then our home was filled with the growing numbers of our permanent families who we called planters. Eager for their first look at the fruits of the *Esperance's* travels through her ports of call, they were not disappointed.

"Come in, friends and neighbors!" my father made all welcome. "See what your feeding of a pious Europe's fasting days has rendered." he called out, offering small tastes of brandy and a bowl of Seville oranges. I turned fine silk handkerchiefs into mischievous bouncing mouses for children of the planter families so their parents could survey plows, rakes, and hoes to assist their growth and harvest seasons ahead. Outside, cattle, sheep, pigs, and chickens waited to be claimed. There was even a surprise for our Randall—chunks of lapis lazuli to grind and add to his images of our deep blue waters and skies.

Darkness descended. My father was perhaps too generous with his brandy and oranges. The last of our visitors lingered. Fishermen delayed settling in their rooms in lodging houses. The supper fires burned and waited. My onion and wild meadow mushroom soup was turning into stew on our own kitchen hearth stones. My good-natured father's eyes finally showed his exhaustion as he slapped the stragglers on their shoulders. "Have mercy, dear neighbors, I've yet to find my land legs!"

But when the fisherfolk, townspeople, and farmers were finally gone, he held me in place. He had one more duty to fulfill. He pulled up a sea chest I recognized. The one he has reserved for me for as long as my memory reached.

Delight replaced the weariness in his eyes. "Remove the first item only," he instructed. "It is a gift from King Louis' court at Versailles."

"Oh, Papa. Madame de Maintenon remembers me?"

"*Mais bien sur.* I am a mere acquaintance from our younger days. You, her bridge between continents, she finds endlessly interesting."

My fingers separated the delicate paper to reveal a square necked gown of exquisite loveliness.

"She married her poet at your age and thinks you should have a proper lady's *attire a la derniere mode.*"

I swept its skirts from the chest and held it up as my father smiled.

"Madame has brought covered shoulders back into fashion, along with classical drapery," he explained. "Ever practical for our climate, she insisted her dressmakers work their magic in wool, not the silks and satins of court. And no headdress accompanies your ensemble, *Petite Onde.* I told her you rarely cover your head in any season. Was she shocked? *Mais non!* She proclaimed it a marvelous idea and left her own fontange off when she sat for her latest portrait. Quite the scandal. But the court of the sun king thrives on scandal."

I held my gift close, enchanted by its softness and simple elegance. "I shall write my thanks to the king's cherished counselor by morning's light. She is a godmother *magnifique.*"

"Aye. To you and her school of female scholars who will help guide the history of France for the next hundred years, it is to be hoped. Just as the king's sponsored brides *les filles du roi* have thrived and doubled the population of Canada. But this will come about only if Madame can marry off her wonders of creation to men of influence who will open trade and not wars among us."

"What of the wars, Papa?"

"On board the *Esperance,* we sail around them, exchanging our cod for their goods as we have for generations, hoping they will keep us out of their disputes."

"It is devoutly to be hoped."

He leaned over and pressed his lips to my forehead. "You are my hope, *Petite Onde,* growing straight and tall, like the one who bore you. And full of her open heart." He stepped back and his earring gave out a merry little sound. He laughed. "Our

Madame de Maintenon also included a treatise on the Beatitudes and the latest folio of Mr. Shakespeare's plays and sonnets in your gift chest as well. Be sure to study both and write that your religious and literary education is not being neglected."

"Ho, am I one of her brides then?"

"No. You are not one of Madame's attempts to save the old world. You are her hope for the new."

"New? The Keepers of the Dawn have been here since before the time of the giant rabbit and beaver hunts."

"Aye, you have caught this old Jerseyman out with this observation. But Charlotte Jaddore has never been here before," he contended. "Set on this earth to match wits with her poor weary father."

He fell into his bed soon after, leaving most of his steaming bowl, along with bread and cheese untouched. He stayed abed until morning's light. Did he find a peaceful rest, breathing in the lavender I'd sprinkled among his sheets? Of this I doubt. Well, it was enough to have him returned, his dear presence in my life again, even if I could hear him still steering his ship around the Atlantic's icebergs in his sleep.

Chapter 2
To Salem

Three days later I came in from my morning visit to our garden shrine to Our Lady in the arms of her mother Saint Anne, where I gave thanks and some breadcrumbs to her birds for my father's return.

I found him at our kitchen's trestle table, finishing my codfish pie and reading missives from his tin letter box. I caught the scent of salt sea spray about him. Where had he been?

He rose when he saw me and kissed my forehead. "Your cooking improves."

"Or perhaps, after a month at sea, it is your appetite that has improved?"

"A contributing factor, only. Charlotte, how fare my mother and grandmother and our relations inland?"

I loved how he regarded my mother's people as his own and never spoke with cumbersome "In-law" attachments. "All are thriving," I assured him. "And, have you yet considered the contents of our relatives' storage baskets? There are fine pelts to trade for needles and cooking pots."

His eyebrow rose, disappearing into the unruly brown curls at his forehead. "Are those the basis of my worth to those hard bargaining women?"

"A contributing factor only."

He laughed. "It is good to be home."

"Hmm," I considered. "For now."

"Why, daughter of my heart, what do you insinuate?"

I nodded toward the cache of missives that had come for him off fleet sailing ketches from our south, the lands of our New England trading partners. "You left cargo in the hold of the *Esperance*. Are other ports calling for a visit before fishing season begins in earnest?"

"Other ports, yes. His smile turned sad. "And a family obligation, *ma cherie*."

"Family, Papa?"

"I have received a letter from Phillippe—Philip."

"Ah." I remembered. "Our cousin who changed his name."

"Indeed. My mother was born a L'Anglois, as was Philippe. He translated his name to Philip English soon after settling in Massachusetts Bay Colony."

"You did not, here in this English colony. Why did he?"

"We were both born Jerseymen, but his adopted community in Massachusetts Bay is not like ours."

"How is this?"

"Well, it is not so filled by people with differences."

"But they trade with the wider world around, like us?"

"They do." His fine brow knit in concentration, as it always did when he strove to explain a difficult thing. "Yet the ones of Philippe's home, they are ruled by people who came early in this waning century, and by the precepts of their religion."

"Ah. They are called Puritans, these people?"

"They are called this by their enemies, yes. Puritans seek to purify the Christianity of the old religion.

"Old religion? Do you mean the religion of the Mi'kmaq? Also, my religion, Catholic?"

"Well, the English form of it, yes, called Anglican. Others want to separate themselves. The Puritans and Separatists are people who have great influence over the lives of all inhabitants. They are very pious, but restrictive." Now something else took over his face—indignation. "Their ancestors burned the paintings of Botticelli and closed the theaters of Shakespeare."

My father has seen the wonders of Lisbon, Florence, Rome and London as well as the salons of Paris and King Louis' court at Versailles. "Grave sins," I concluded.

"Are you teasing me, daughter?" he demanded with a mocking affront.

"*Pas du tout*. Not at all," I assured him. "Is it not a sin to deny the beauty that flows from Master Shakespeare's pen or the vibrant new color you have brought for our dear town crier's brush?"

"Added to the fine red dyes of our relatives the Beothuk, who also understand how to see what is beautiful? Yes, to deny the beautiful is exactly that, a sin. But these people are seldom concerned with the beauty of the world. They see devils everywhere. And they mistrust the French of Canada and Acadie and their native allies, who have raided settlements in Maine when they encroached on the land of the Wabanaki peoples. We are deeper in wartime this year, *ma petite onde*."

I felt a coldness wash over me like a wave, for I fear war worse than any plague. "Not here. Not among us, Papa!"

"No," he said softly, as if he were trying to convince himself as well as me. "We will not allow this European war of King William to come between us and our friends. This island is both Newfoundland and *Terre-Neuve*, is it not? Even this small part, this peninsula holds St. John's and Placentia settlements both, no? We will not allow the wars of religion. They are of times past. They are of other places, older places, these wars. Not in the new world, where we learn from each other, where we love each other, as I loved the one who was your mother. But it is not the same to our south, in Massachusetts

Bay Colony. These are people who are ruled by, not our fondest hopes, but by their fear, my darling. And now they have turned these fears on each other."

"Papa, your mothers were sisters. How did our cousin come to be among such people?"

His brows slanted in sad amusement. "The same way the wandering seaman you see before you came to be here, darling girl. "He fell in love."

"With a Puritan lady."

"*Exactement, ma chère.*"

"What does our cousin write to you in his letter, Papa?"

"Of a passing strange season that has overtaken his community, which is called Salem. A season of witches."

"Witches? The healing women the West Country fishermen speak of? The ones who they went to for ailment cures and love potions, and sometimes, for predictions of events to come?"

"No. This is a darker business. It began over this winter past, in a minister's household, with the ravings of children."

"Ravings?"

"Yes. Similar to such things that went on in stories the minister reads to these very children- about Boston preacher Cotton Mather's examination of a poor laundress a few years ago—stories of invisible, spectral torments that he was convinced caused rants and ravings. But the strange behavior worsened when Mather took the victims into his own household to be cured." My father shook his head. "Probably some children frightened by an admonition or afflicted with a palsy."

"What happened to the woman accused? The laundress?"

"The reverend called her obstinate in her idolatry. She was an Irish Catholic, who escaped Cromwell's persecutions, but not those of Massachusetts Bay. She was hanged as a witch."

"Poor lady."

"None but your generous heart would call Ann Glover a lady. For them she was a woman who sometimes spoke in the language that she was born into—Irish. She could recite the Lord's Prayer in Irish and Latin, but not English. She was poor, past her childbearing years, and a widow, without a man to speak up for her, only that Boston preacher badgering her to repent her witchcraft or forfeit her life."

"My grandmothers say that lying is worse than dying."

"Yes, *ma cher*. The laundress would have made a good Beothuk or Mi'kmaq it seems. She stood firm and did not repent. Mather warned that more witchcraft would follow. He wrote a book to be a guide for when God's displeasure with his chosen lets loose witches on the land. Now the people of Salem see witches in the woods surrounding them and across their own household's tables and even during their religious services. They have jailed not only the poor and defenseless, but revered grandmothers and a child of four years who pronounced herself the minion of her mother. They even hunt for and speak of putting one of their own former ministers to his death, imagine! Philip fears the same fate will befall his Mary."

"His pious lady wife?"

He shook his head sadly. "We thought we had left this behind in our old world."

"Papa, what can we do?"

"Philip asks us to come to Salem, with provisions for his neighbors who have suffered a hard winter. To remind them of who he is, and how his trading adds to their own prosperity. He seeks to get back into their good graces. And show that his family belongs among them. That the English name was once L'Anglois, yes, but is not in league with devils."

"Why would they think such things?"

"Because he is an immigrant to these shores, and now, a rich one, thanks to his efforts, and his marriage alliance. He has had land disputes with neighbors. The neighbors have won these suits, but still hold tight to their grudges. And Philip has a wife whose childbearing years are coming to an end. And her own widowed, tavern-keeper mother was herself accused of witchcraft in years gone by."

"What became of this lady?"

"She was acquitted and sued her accusers for their slander."

"And won this suit?"

"And won."

"Surely her daughter might win again."

"Philip fears things are different now, thanks to these hard times, and the war, and Cotton Mather and his book. Philip has called on us, his family, with urgency. An urgency that supersedes my duties as fishing admiral. Our Randall is rendering all the built-up cases to documents to be judged upon my return. I have convinced our neighbors to await the next incoming ships so I might gain my vice and rear admirals to consult with on judgements. And we needs must gather wisdom from among your mother's people, for one of the complaints concerns them."

"Aye. Animosities have been gathering the winter long here."

"So I understand. Disputes that need must be settled. But, Charlotte, Philip English's belief in me made the *Esperance* and all that followed in our prosperity possible."

"You will sail for Salem then? Soon?" I hoped my disappointment did not show in my voice.

"I have been up on the cliffs before dawn. The winds are right, with crested waves in the bay."

"Spray on the ocean? This day, then?"

"Aye, daughter." His brows slanted in amusement. What was this? He is not a cruel man, my father. He would not find joy in my distress, would he? His next words gave me my answer. "Fancy a run up the rigging?"

"I might come? Aboard the *Esperance*?"

"If you can find your britches and tie up your glorious hair. I have my duty to our cousin, but cannot part with you so soon."

"But what of the store? And your crew... they have not found their land legs."

He laughed. "Spoken like a merchant's daughter! I have not yet lost you to the Beothuk and the Mi'kmaq! Randall Kelly has agreed to forego his artistic pursuits and add storekeeping to his scribe and town crier duties. And I have already bargained for the return of at least a skeleton crew of men more at home on the sea."

"And who are beyond loyal to a good captain."

"Not so good that bonus pay and rations of figs and limes both were not required."

I grinned. "Overfond of limes too, I am."

"You see? My own daughter robs me!"

I threw my arms around him. "How can I rob a man who never sleeps?"

His laughing eyes sobered. "Charlotte. You must pack Madame de Maintenon's gift, the grey gown. And wear it in Salem, under the plainest of your cloaks. The gown is beautiful, but also modest and devout, like our gracious queen. It will be your armor."

"Armor, papa?"

"Yes. I fear for you, sometimes, my love. In this world that men have made."

* * *

My sailor's togs felt as natural on me as a second skin. I kept only my medicine bag from my island life, its soft deerskin ties around my neck instead of at my middle. As I braided and pinned my hair under a peaked seaman's cap, my father's crew welcomed me aboard with my favorite of their work songs.

Cape Cod girls, they use no combs
Heave away! Haul away!
They sort their hair with codfish bones
Heave away, haul away!
And we're bound for Megansett!

I had lived the winter with my mother's people, so there was no need for any toughening of limbs. The ropes felt good in my hands and under my feet. The crew, Jerseymen all, like my father, called me *Petite Onde*, my childhood name, while on board. I felt myself to be that child again among them. For our days at sea I was not on the brink of womanhood, with obligations to household, our island community, and as a bridge person between them and the Mi'kmaq and Beothuk. I was a sailor, with duties only to our ship and gracious captain, as he navigated us through familiar swells and coastlines to the south of the American continent. It was smooth and beautiful sailing. I held those days close to my heart in the troubled times ahead.

Chapter 3
Salem's Children

The buildings of Salem town were straight, severe and dark, so unlike the rambling and slope-roofed houses I'd known on St. John's, or the *mamateeks*, white birch covered fir pole homes of my inland relatives. The many-gabled English house of my father's cousin, within view of the harbor on Essex Street, was so grand I thought it a tavern or community building, not the abode of a single family. We were led by lantern light to a spacious room with a hearth and table set with a welcoming meal of cornbread and mutton stew.

"My master bids you rest and take refreshment," the household's cook, a young widow named Goodwife Witheridge whispered with a curtsey before she disappeared again. I felt my father and I had come out of the fog and into an old tale. Perhaps Philip English was transformed into one of Salem's many roaming devils and would soon appear out of the flames of the fire with his book for us to sign. Were we to become part of his pack of Salem witches?

From whence had those thoughts come? From my ponderings on the Reverend Cotton Mather's book? His instructions on what to do when Satan and his witches invaded Massachusetts Bay colony? This was not the time or place for macabre humor. But the air itself carried a miasma of danger, suspicion, and fear, it seemed.

We waited. "Our cousin offers hospitality," my father said uneasily.

"In peculiar form."

"This whole town is peculiar."

Had he felt it too? Did it originate from the stares we'd both received since we'd left the *Esperance*? Stares that said, who was this strange dark creature by my tall and handsome father's side? One bold enough to wear a fine French gown, however modestly cut? Did the captain of the *Esperance* have a daughter by a Portuguese mistress? Or...worse, was she his by a woman who was a godless native of these shores?

We ate in silence the well-prepared meal, and a cornbread nearly as good as that of my grandmothers. So, these Puritans did learn something from the people they now called savages, people who had once welcomed and sustained them. But where was our host?

Once we'd finished our meal my father stood, walked about the room in ponderous, clodding steps so different from his fleet-footedness aboard his beloved ship. Soon came the return of Goodwife Witheridge and a tray set with a green bottle and three stemmed glasses. She nodded. "Might you partake in Madeira wine?"

"If one of those foretells our kinsman's presence," my father said quietly.

A small smile was his reward. The woman brought her tray and bid us follow her silent steps to a room that contained the kitchen hearth. She moved so quietly I wondered if Philip English's servant housekeeper had garnered more than cooking skills from friends of the forest. She pressed her palm against a wooden panel to reveal a door that slid behind another. There appeared a small space within, with barely room to stand. It contained a yoke backed chair and small table. And a man who resembled my father in coloring and the firm set of his jaw. But our cousin was older, with streaks of grey mixed with the brown hair at his temples. His form was also more heavy-set than my angular seaman father.

"You see before you the lately elected town selectman's fall from grace to ... this, cousin," Philip English said in a voice roughened with anger.

Goodwife Witheridge gave us all a small curtsey. "I shall keep watch, sir," she promised, before leaving us.

The sons of the Jaddore sisters moved slowly toward each other. They took each other's hands, then grasped their forearms.

Our cousin spoke first. "*Mon capitaine.* You have brought food provisions?"

Papa nodded. "Now stored it in the warehouse you directed us to."

"*Merci bien.* It will not bring hardship to St. John's?"

"No. It was a good year. On land and at sea." My father looked deeply into his cousin's eyes. "We are so sorry for your troubles here."

Philip took in a halting breath, but only a soft, guttural sound came out of him.

They embraced- a full, holding embrace of love. "Some respect the ties of kinship," Philip whispered.

"And kindnesses, and opportunity," my father said into his shoulder.

"Nonsense," his cousin objected with a small laugh that made his face more like my father's. "It was a good business decision to enfold a young pirate into the more legitimate society of my merchant fleet captains."

My father stepped back and placed his hand on my shoulder. "Cousin, this is my daughter, Charlotte," he introduced me.

I saw no disdain in Philip English's eyes, only wonder. "Full of a fierce compassion I think, this one. There is a chance for them, then?"

"Who, sir?" I asked.

"The children. All but our Susanna, who suffers too greatly without her mother and abides with her in prison."

My father's swift intake of breath sharpened the air. "Your lady wife has been accused? Taken?"

"Oh yes. Our sheriff, a despicable lout with his hand in every pocket, came for her in the dead of night. Mary refused to go with him until morning, so she could prepare the children and our household of servants. She stood her ground. My accomplished, delicate Mary, imagine! And she stood up to her accusers at Judge Corwin's house the next day. It made no difference. I could only bribe her away from our filthy jail, now overcrowded with unfortunates. This town has become a madhouse, cousins. Mary now abides in a Boston prison under better conditions. I remained free, working to exert my influence to have her freed. Then they came for me. Thanks to our good lady housekeeper, I learned Corwin and his crew were coming, and she hid me in this room, like the priest holes of the Old World's wars of religion, eh, cousin?"

My father's grim smile was his answer.

"Our children whom I seek to entrust into your care are three," our cousin continued. "Mary, who is in her fifteenth year, Philip, who is seven, and our toddling child William who has achieved but two years."

"Are they in this house, sir?" I asked.

"They are being brought here by trusted neighbors. But I know not for how long even they can remain loyal, can be trusted. Or when they catch the fever of recrimination and greed that has infested so many others. Might you sail our children away to your

36

home on Newfoundland, until this plague of the mind has passed and we might be reunited? If the worst happens, will you make my family your own, cousins? So that some part of us might move on through the generations? Remember our Shakespeare sonnets, Martin? 'You had a father; let your son say so', eh? They are good children, and will mind you, Cousin Charlotte, they—"

My father held up his hand. "Stop, stop, Philippe. Of course."

"We will take them into our home and hearts." I tried to further assure our cousin. "But might we not provide a home for you all?"

"I fear not, my dear. If it even could be accomplished, that will make their mother and I criminals. I see the greedy eyes of some of my neighbors differently now. I thought it was mere envy, of one not like them amassing wealth. They think I wed Mary for her father's money, they think us too lavish in our ways. I am a foreigner to them, and not even the right kind of Protestant. But Mary is a fulsome member of the congregation that now persecutes her and little Susanna both! I cannot abandon them. I must keep working to get them freed." His doleful eyes changed then, as if lit from within. "I will bring suits against all her tormentors, starting with the Corwins, mark me! And that rotter Beal, who once accused my dear mother-in-law, and now says I am making his nose gush red with blood. With him it was so much more than envy. They covet this house, my ships and my wharves as they coveted my mother-in-law's tavern a generation ago. That good woman warned me of this on her deathbed, that the stirrings of this evil were again in the land. But in the arrogance of my manhood, my wealth, I did not heed."

A small rhythmic knock came from the room's door. A smile appeared on the beleaguered man's face. "Ah, blessings on my clever housekeeper and her signals. Come meet my children."

And so, our guardianship began. Standing dockside, the three English children seemed a smaller family, with fair-haired Elizabeth and William trying mightily to be the parents of the smiling child still in his toddling dress who was bestowing farewell kisses on the face of his father. I saw a gap too, between their parents' namesakes, a gap where other children had been, children other than the one who languished in a prison cell with her mother, I thought. This family has had losses, has been scarred by past sorrows, too, like my own.

Once aboard, the younger Philip English threw back the slight shoulders of his four-foot frame once he had assessed the *Esperance* and its crew.

"Are these few men and this flimsy bark expected to bear us across the waves of the Atlantic?" he demanded.

I felt my cheeks burn with indignation, but my father laughed and nodded to his helmsman, Mr. Pike. "She has plowed three oceans, young squire, and been thrice set afire by pirates off the Barbary coast!"

"Burned?" our cousin asked, fear invading his imperious tone.

"Nay! Scorched only, Now, 'twas the *Black Raven* we burned to the water line. Eh, boys?"

My father's seamen agreed, sounding like pirates themselves.

Joseph Picard, our bosun, stepped forward, throwing my cap at me. "Besides, with young Charlotte at the rigging and in the crow's nest with her spyglass, we're a full complement crew for coastal duty. Into your togs, sailor!" he ordered.

That put an end to my cousin's critical appraisal of the *Esperance*. It also left both he and Mary in wide-eyed silence. Only Will continued to babble about the "pretty birds" flying above our masts.

And he was the only one of the three to come near me that night, still dressed in my crewmate's attire. He even took some warm oat porridge from the spoon I held to his lips.

"Where Mama?" he asked me.

I looked up at his sister, whose eyes filled with tears.

"On an adventure with your papa and Susanna," I told him. "Just as you and Mary and Philip are, with us. Oh, the stories we'll have to tell each other, yes? When we are all together again?"

"Stories?"

"Aye, laddie." I said, falling into my storyteller voice. "Would you like to hear one now?"

He nodded his sleepy head and left his little stool for my lap.

"Is there a little toy or poppet for him in your belongings?" I asked his siblings.

Philip looked somehow frightened by my request, but his sister's head shot up and her lips pressed together. "Certainly not!"

"We believe such things are distractions," Philip further explained.

Mary sighed hard as she looked out at the waves. "What have we done wrong? Where and with whom has our father sent us out to?" she asked them. Then her shoulders slumped, and she leaned her head on her hand.

Little William snuggled under my heart. "Do you know how the deer got her spots?" I asked him.

"No. Tell me, Cousin Car-lot," he implored.

"Well, long, long ago..." and we were off on the first story my Mi'kmaq grandmother told me when I was his age.

Chapter 4
Return To St. John's

"Where is your meeting house?"

"We have none."

"But, from whence does your minister preach?"

"We have none of those either," my father supplied the answer, this time, relieving me.

"But we are not without services," I offered. "When a ship of the royal navy puts in at harbor, we ask their chaplain to conduct services, weddings, and baptisms."

"Anglican chaplains?"

"Well, yes."

The look of continued horror on my cousin's face kept me from mentioning the occasional visits we enjoyed from Catholic missionary priests that lived among the Mi'kmaq.

I was happy when we arrived on our doorstep.

"This is not so fine a house as ours," Mary observed as her gaze went into the rafters. She held herself erect and tall. I wondered if it was in imitation of her mother. "How many servants keep it?"

My father and I exchanged glances. "We... hire on some help at spring and fall cleaning time," I said.

Once inside, I managed to keep my voice even as I tried to remember my manners. It was hard for me with Mary, who was closer to my own age. The bluster of seven-year-old Philip was easier. And I was most glad toddling William and I had taken to each other over our return to St. John's. He now lost himself in my skirts the way he'd played in the sails I mended nightly aboard ship.

"Our import goods have a place below with the kitchen and scullery. Sleeping quarters are on the upper floor - Papa's chamber in the middle and the others on either side," I further explained our simple household, wondering what she would think upon learning she was to share my sleeping chamber, that now held crates and boxes of trade goods as well in the large space.

Mary pursed her lips. "We shall have to mind William on the stairs, if there are no servants," she observed.

"Of course."

She lifted the linen curtain and glanced out the window, frowning towards the declaiming person and his bell. "Does that man need to be so boisterous?"

"Randall is our crier."

"A lame town crier? Who is so loud he renders us all deaf? Is this place mad?"

Madder than the place that takes your mother for a witch? The words almost flew from my lips before my father's warning eye caught mine.

Papa laughed. "Randall Kelly is a renaissance man of many talents besides his effective voice, cousin. He cries out your presence among us. That might well attract a few visitors to welcome you to our island, perhaps. And goodwife pies."

I nodded. "Papa raised up Randall and I together since we were children."

My cousin's lips pursed again. "Ah. This may explain clouded judgement."

My father's cough was dry. "Perhaps Charlotte could show you up the stairs, young ones?"

Mary finally turned from the window. "First we must make a prayer of thanksgiving for our safe arrival, must we not, Cousin Martin?"

My father's voice, if not his startled eyes, recovered quickly. "A prayer? Yes, yes, a wonderful idea! Would you like to lead us?"

It was her turn to be surprised. "Is this a Quaker-influenced household, where women preach?"

Now I felt I needs must rescue her from the impatience developing in my father's eyes. "No preachers here," I said. "But we all pray, do we not, Cousin Mary?"

"In thanksgiving," my father recovered the kindness in his voice as he raised his glance heavenward, "to Jesus our Lord, who when there were brought unto him little children, that he should put his hands on them, and pray: and the disciples rebuked them. But Jesus said, 'Suffer little children, and forbid them not, to come unto me: for of such is the kingdom of heaven.'"

While the children's heads were still bowed, my father's shoulder touched mine as he leaned close to my ear. "Saint Matthew to the rescue," he breathed out, before reaching for his hat. "And now I must give thanks to my crew with their pay," he announced, and headed for the door.

The coward.

Little William pulled at my skirts. "Pies?" he asked.

Chapter 5
Before the Court of the Fishing Admirals

Over the next few days our curious neighbors took stock of our Salem relations. Through my cousins' eyes I began to see our growing community differently, as a stranger would. Our planters were people who had decided to winter over, sending for their families to join them. Some now had fishing stations of their own. They hired on indentured servants, mostly Jersey islanders and West country folk gathered up at county fairs for the journey across the Atlantic. I noticed the different complexions of laughing seasonal fisherfolk who greeted our cousins too. Most different of all, of course, were a few of our Mi'kmaq allies, who fished in their own coves, and brought us trade goods from the interior—pelts to keep us warm in winter, the meat of the sacred caribou. Its ancient name was *tuktu*—the one who feeds us. Only their kin the Beothuk did not appear in our sturdy house, as they had long ago chosen to avoid contact with people who had sailed into their homeland from the places beyond where dawn rose.

"How long ago?" I once asked my Beothuk Grandmother Demas.

"Since the horned ones, who came in great canoes with sea monsters at their helm."

"Greenlanders? Icelanders? Vikings?"

"Many names for the same people. We wanted nothing to do with them. Or any that came after. So we learned how to live inside this island, fishing the trout in the lakes, and away from all the tall ships, and the greed of people out of balance." She touched my face. "You dwell among them, Loved by the Waters. We fear for you."

Soon people came for my father to render judgements in matters that had built up over the winter season. There was no judicial body in our land but the fishing admirals. My father was joined by the captains who'd arrived second and third in the harbor. Captain Worthing, whose fleet ship which he captured in the Dutch wars sailed the Mediterranean, was this year's Vice-Admiral. He was a man built square and strong, whose deep listening and hearty laugh charmed all, especially the womenfolk of St. John's. Captain Lacey commanded the *Calcutta*, a ship of the East India Company laden with cotton, cinnamon, nutmeg and silks. His hair was a flame of red and he always carried the scent of the spices he traded—spices that enhanced our pork and mutton feasts with the tastes of the world. Captain Lacey took on Rear Admiral duties. Both of my father's fellow judges were more than a decade senior of his own thirty-seven years. Still, they looked to him for final judgement on disputes of all levels of consequence.

A disappointed fourth ship's commander in harbor was Josiah Dunbar, captain of The *Countess Amelia*, which was also the name of the lady who was his betrothed, a noblewoman who had estates in England and Bermuda as well as lands here on Avalon. Captain Dunbar called both woman and ship "my countess" sometimes leading to confusion. He was closer to my father's age, but there the resemblance ended. My father's stance and dress was closer to the fishermen. Because of our frequent wet weather, he favors clothing of cotton, linen and wool, which all dry quickly. He carefully fringed the ends of his outerwear like our native allies to wick off the rain, and he prefers moccasins over leather boots. Captain Dunbar stood sturdier than my father's angular form, especially dressed in the latest of the English nautical fashions of his station: cocked hat, brocaded waistcoat and breeches with garters about the knees, blue coat that reached his hip, bucked shoes and his gleaming silver sword at his hip.

Captain Dunbar had charge of a growing estate called Adlington Manor. It looked over the head of the harbor on the cliffs, near the lands of the Brewster family's Raven Hill. George Wyatt's small farm nestled between them. Both neighbors tried to buy his farm every spring, but thus far Master Wyatt had them raise prices against each other, until he refused them both. Our cousins Mary and Philip said that such land squabbles reminded them of home, except that ours were a source of amusement, and Salem's looked to be turning deadly.

Josiah Dunbar made a great show of getting our neighbors to set up defensive fortifications overlooking the harbor, to be ready for the French attack he was sure was coming by sea. But the only attacks so far in King William's war were our own navy raids against the French at Plaisance. Captain Dunbar was the only person of St. John's who had a personal servant, an African man named Primus, who stood at his master's height, and dressed in the same brocaded clothing, only a little more threadbare. He'd fished with Randall and I when we were children, enchanting us with stories of his life on Bermuda in his deep, musical voice. But lately he'd kept himself distant from all but his duties at his master's side. A hardness had replaced the laughter around his eyes.

Soon we learned there would be no more ships from French ports. The English king had forbidden it. Our sheltering harbor, once welcoming the shipping world, was not the bustling place it had been in years past. It would be a lean year ahead.

Our fishing court met to discuss how we were to get through the war. And how long might it last. What had it to do with us? Our trade was with the world around. We did not understand the sources of the conflict of nations. Thanks to familiar waterways, we were much closer to our colonial neighbors in New France than our fellow English colonies to the south. The pirates would take advantage of the warfare too, and take their plunder from all sides.

The war brought talk of deprivations and of facing hardships, but the fishing admirals' court also served as amusement as well as civic duty. Cases were heard inside the Sea Parrot tavern. Among our neighbors sat Mary and me on that first calling of the court, while Philip and William joined the other children on the green outside, under a welcome warm spring day. I'm not sure I had convinced their disapproving sister that the races the children were running in sport were necessary to make their limbs ready for steering the plow at planting.

I leaned forward as my father listened to the disputes set before him. He and his admirals served our community well. Their judgements turned perceived slights into forgiven misunderstandings. The admirals helped debtors work out repayment schedules and limited the late-night hours of the four Welsh brothers' boisterous harmonies under Mrs. Ridley's window as she set her twins down for their afternoon slumbers.

As the day's proceedings ended, Captain Dunbar made a great show of congratulating the court and inviting my father and his admirals to remain at the tavern and dine with him to celebrate. I could tell my father was reluctant to accept, especially as a joyous William leapt into his arms to show him his ball, a gift from one of the race-running children.

Captain Dunbar leaned his fine gloved hand on the hilt of his sword. "Surely your able daughter and this fine Massachusetts Bay maiden can settle the family for the evening, Martin?" he asked as he slapped my father's back. Why did I feel it was more of a challenge than an assurance?

Mary took her brother from my father's arms. "We are able indeed sir, as we come from a merchant household ourselves, and well understand our duties."

"Your father's name is well known to us, Mistress English. And it is devoutly to be hoped that your family's troubles may be ended soon."

"I thank you, sir," she answered with a small curtsey. "With the help of a just, almighty God."

"And actions of his elect."

A look of recognition came over Mary's face, as if she'd found a kindred spirit in this heathen wilderness at last. "Indeed, sir," she intoned, with a deeper curtsy.

Chapter 6
Captain Dunbar's Proposal

And so we lost our father's good company for the evening, and even further into the night. Only I was still awake by our main room's fireside when both my father and Captain Dunbar, leaning on his servant Primus's arm, entered our home.

My father's hospitable nature was still in evidence as he asked me to fetch small glasses and a bottle of his favorite digestive. Ah, that is how Josiah Dunbar wheedled his way into our house so late, I thought, a complaint of illness after dining? I hoped Papa's offer of a cure signaled it was time to bring their evening to a close.

At first the choice of drink provoked an argument. "Why, Captain Jaddore-- you offer me eau-de-vie without the water that turns it back into wine? Its flavor is vile!"

"Not anymore," my father assured him. "The Dutch have tried a second distilling in the city of Cognac. The French have refined it more fully. Then barrels containing the wine have been left abandoned for months, and nothing less than a miracle has happened. Please, sit." My father invited his guest.

Primus eased his master down into our best turned chair, then disappeared into the room's shadows.

I poured two glasses. "Thank you, Charlotte. Taste," he urged his guest.

He did. A wide smile crept over Josiah Dunbar's face. "I see."

"Others will too, it is to be hoped. Once the French ports are opened to us again."

"You pirate!"

"I am a merchant seaman, sir. At war with no one," my father protested, then took a small sip from his own glass.

"How much of this did you escape with, before the order went out?"

"A good supply," was all Papa conceded.

Captain Dunbar held out his emptied glass. "If you would, Mistress?"

My father nodded. I complied and stepped back. The captain's smile widened as he finished another draught. "Primus," he called, looking behind him, "I am feeling more robust. Bring the horses around," he commanded.

Primus nodded and cast me a slight shake of the head before walking out the door.

"Feeling better?" my father asked his guest.

"I am, sir."

"You will sleep well now, I am sure."

But Captain Dunbar ignored the hint. "We must join forces, my friend. And build more ships."

"More ships?"

"Aye, fleet ones, like yours, of Bermuda cedar. My countess has an estate there, as you know. Let King William have his American oak for his warships for strength and lumbering along on the high seas. We merchants need speed. We need cedar timbered ships, Martin! With deep holds."

"Deep holds are not necessary for the salted cod. Or for our return with silks, wines, fruits, and, in future peaceful times, cognac."

Captain Dunbar lowered his voice. "Deep holds are for human cargo. Picture it, Martin. A great fortune to be made through your cognac and my slave trading."

"Slaves?"

"Aye, man! It is already my practice to take the salted cod that none of the other merchants want to feed the slaves of Jamacia. But there will be a bigger fortune to be made!"

My father's finger traced the side of his glass. "My routes cover the North Atlantic."

"Among nations always at war? Enforcing their restrictions with their warships? Stealing our sailors away from us to fight for them? That is the past, my friend. Surely you are not ignorant of the gathering waters of the slavers. That is the future... Africans of Senegambia! To work on the sugar plantations of the Caribbean and the tobacco fields of Virginia. To be seasoned into high-priced domestic servants like my Primus."

Captain Dunbar noticed my presence by the door and directed his next remark towards me. "Let not the rambling dreams of two seafarers keep you from your slumbers, good lady," he proclaimed.

I looked to my father, who rose and bowed formally to me. "Thank you for your gracious offerings, Charlotte. I will set all to right and bank the fires. Take your rest." But his look told me to leave my chamber door ajar. I took my leave and climbed the stairs. Listening to their continued conversation was easily achieved.

"Josiah. When will Primus be ending his term of indenture?" Ah. If his guest would not leave, Papa took it upon himself to at least steer their conversation.

His companion's voice lowered. "I have a life servant now."

"He has accepted this arrangement?"

"He has no choice in the matter."

"How is that?"

"The laws of Bermuda have been changed. Indentures are extended."

"Extended? But indentures are contracted. How far extended?"

"To ninety-nine years."

"That is not possible! Why, if we broke bond with our servants here, they would mutiny. It cannot be different in Bermuda."

"Terms have been extended only for our African servants."

My fingers went to my mouth to stifle a gasp. No wonder about the changes in our fishing companion's demeanor.

"Ninety-nine years is a lifetime," my father said softly.

Primus's master laughed. "Unless they are very healthy. And my Primus is. He may see his freedom yet, eh?"

I heard the strain in my father's voice. "Does he have knowledge of his new status, sir?"

"Do not trouble yourself so, my friend! Primus sees me as his father."

"And are you his father, sir?"

Had Papa overindulged in his own cognac, I wondered, to say such a thing. But Captain Dunbar only laughed. "Is that what is rumored? Because of the lightness of my African's skin?"

"It is," my father acknowledged.

"My goodness towards him must have led to such talk. I have kept him close, seasoned him to perfection, eh? He has no desire to be free of me. If I allow him to marry, I can dangle possible freedom for his children, who I cannot legally hold in bondage. Not yet. But we masters make the laws, do we not? And we can change them."

I heard him empty another glass down his throat. "Martin Jaddore, what is in this French witches' brew of yours?"

"There is no witchcraft in this house."

"No, no of course not! So serious of a sudden, my friend! Do not worry. The talk about your expanded Salem-bred household and your dusky daughter is only West Country nonsense among the fisherfolk, and planters weaving their tales and grudges over the long winter. You and your admirals will put all to rights. Then we can get on to further discussion of our business together. A most pleasant warmth from this concoction, sir."

"It is stronger than eau-de-vie, I warned you."

"Indeed you did. You are an honest man. That will be to my benefit in our partnership. Your reputation as a fair trader. The rest you must leave to me."

"The rest?"

"The rest will be lucrative for us both. When my countess comes, I will introduce you, if you promise not to flash those fine eyes and handsome smile to win her away from me, eh? She can figure in both our futures."

"I do not take your meaning."

"Our dynasties, man! I have set mine afoot: to marry her, to plant a child in her illustrious belly before I take my leave of her most winters. You must think to your own mark left on the world, sir."

His voice became softer then, as if he knew I was listening. But I was trained by my grandmothers. I did not have their full woodland skills, but I knew human voices, and I did not miss a word. "Find yourself a proper English wife, or one of your Madame Maintenon's young, buxom students out of her court ladies' school when the latest war is over, eh? Sire a half dozen boys with her whilst you plow the seas. Soon they will man your ships whilst you rescue black African souls from their pagan worship of darkness and count your share of our profits."

My father's soft, seething voice came next. "And what of Charlotte?"

"Ah. We all make mistakes in our youth. Marry her off to a planter and make your wild daughter another man's problem. Or send her to a convent so she can take the veil and serve the Jesuits among the Mi'kmaq Praying Indians. She is not part of our future together, you must see that, Martin. God's teeth, this is potent. We must raise another glass to the good citizens of Cognac."

"I think you must find your way home, Captain."

My father's tone was as sharp as ice, but his guest remained as jovial as ever. "Indeed," he agreed. "A weariness overtakes me. Where is my Primus? Where is his strong arm, always ready to do my bidding?"

"You sent him out before you told me of his enslavement."

I heard our door open and wondered if it had ever been latched once Primus took leave of his master. "Just here, Captain."

"Ah. I cannot do without you, Primus."

"Yes, sir."

"You are grateful, are you not? Grateful for all the gifts I have bestowed on you, besides the finery that goes from my back to yours. Tell Captain Jaddore. He thinks me heartless."

"Oh, my master has a heart, sir," Primus acknowledged.

I watched from our second story windows as Captain Dunbar, on his servant's arm, turned. "To my Primus, I remain ever without fault. You have that in your daughter, Martin. I understand your devotion to her, truly. But you must be practical. Let her be the saint, serving her people, keeping their arrows from our backs. You must make your fortune, and your posterity's future."

My father was so still I thought he had fallen asleep in his chair when I entered the room with my tray to collect the Cognac and their glasses. But he was staring into the fire. And his eyes were full of tears. He took my hand. "Please, Charlotte," he whispered. "You are my joy. Do not you leave me because of my associations."

I knelt at his feet. "Oh, Papa. I have heard worse. *In vino veritas* is valuable to us both, yes?"

"Aye. And now I know Captain Dunbar's mind. But at what cost? Poor Primus. I know it is said to be a common occurrence in the warmer colonies, but I remain astonished that a man could enslave his own son."

"His master thinks he is invisible, there in the shadows. But Papa, Primus is not invisible, or without ears. And he is not Captain Dunbar's son."

"Dunbar does not deny it."

"Because it serves his interests, I think. Primus once told Randall and I that he believes himself the son of a seaman-- one who had served out his indenture before Primus was born."

"A free man, then?"

"Yes, and one of their Bermuda household once told him that his mother, too, was free--an Irish woman he barely remembers."

"Does she live?"

"Nay, long dead now. He endures his servitude in hopes of finding proof of his status. If he does, might he bring it before your court?"

"I will find out if this is possible."

"He has taught himself to read, Papa. And Randall taught him to write."

My father smiled. "The least he can do for a countryman."

"Indeed."

"I should have known you two have learned all this."

"Among those like us, trust can be found. Although Primus no longer counts himself our friend, I fear."

"Well, his mistrust of all of us is well-founded. As for the search for documents that prove Primus a freeman. I find myself in the Bermudas upon occasion, and I have associates I can write to there. Might I join in your efforts?"

"*Mais bien sur.* You would prove a powerful ally."

"I never wish to be the partner that Captain Dunbar envisions. You are my heir and most beloved daughter. You know that, Charlotte?"

"I do, Papa." I kissed his cheek. "I also know it is no dishonor to my mother for you to find love again."

He grunted softly. "No more matchmaking schemes, tonight, if you please. *Mon Dieu*, but that man is vile." He squeezed my hand before rising from his chair and heading up the stairs.

The next morning had Randall Kelly flying into our presence, using his walking stick to launch himself through the kitchen doorway. I continued stirring oats for William's porridge.

"Charlotte." He summoned, "I knew nothing of it! If others did, they must have been bribed to keep it from me!"

I laughed at his even-more-than-usual disheveled form. "A scandal you have learned about later than others? Something I need to know even before our crier rings it out with his bell? Sit down, Randall. It cannot be so serious."

He sat, then stood, then sat again. William clapped, thinking it a game, I think.

"Yes, yes, of course, not serious!" Randall agreed, "Ridiculous, even. But he is pressing forward with the suit. Is he mad?"

"Who? Is who mad?"

"But...but that is how we will tell your father of it, exactly! That is how we will frame it, so that he does not strangle him!"

"Who?"

"George Wyatt!"

"And why would Papa want to strangle Farmer Wyatt?

"Because today you stand accused, Charlotte."

"Accused?"

"Yes! Of witchcraft."

Chapter 7
Accused

George Wyatt came into the tavern Sea Parrot, with his housemaid, his cow, and his butter churn to make his complaint against me. The maid did the best she could to calm the poor cow, as she was not used to being under a strange roof with so much human company. At a time before our journey to Salem, it might have been a source of amusement for all attending the hearing. But even the fine weather turned sour on that suddenly raining, windswept day.

My father's vacant chair was flanked by his vice and rear admirals' seats. But it was there, reminding all that he had made the choice to leave the judgement against his daughter to his companion judges. He did not absent himself from the proceedings, taking a place on the bench beside me.

Farmer Wyatt eyed the assembled crowd, scanning the back wall's standing observers, before nodding and taking his place. When the murmurings had settled, Captain Lacey called my accuser forth. "George Wyatt, on what matter will you be heard?"

"I seek to free my cow of a spell."

Captain Worthing leaned forward. "A spell?"

"Aye. She's been close to dry since Charlotte Jaddore came to treat my servant's sore arm." He pointed at me. "Made sore by that one's blinking my churn. I would ask the judges to press her to remove her curse on both—churn and cow."

Beside me, my father stiffened in anger, but his fellow admirals merely nodded. The windblown lines sprouting from Captain Lacey's eyes crinkled in amusement as he regarded the farmer's entourage.

"You have brought evidence of your complaint, I see."

"Aye, sirs."

"You will not object if we have requested that the estimable Mrs. Gavin examines the churn."

It was not a question. He called forth the lady. Mrs. Gavin was a bright-eyed widowed woman of middle years who was now housekeeper of the Brewster family's fine house at Raven Hill. She wore a striped homespun skirt with a blue and buff bodice. Her sleeves and cap were trim, neat and proper in appearance. Her butter was the one everyone sought after and drew the highest barter and scrip and even coin. She was a good choice. She came forth with sure and steady steps from her place near the crowded tavern's doors. I'd always admired the skillful beauty of the hand-tatting that edged her apron.

As she passed my father and I, Mrs. Gavin's kind eyes made a quick dart heavenward. It was meant for our notice only I think, but I believe Captain Worthing took note of it as well, as he grunted down something that might have been the beginning of a laugh.

We waited. Mrs. Gavin's assessment of the churn was not long in coming. "Ill-made stave fittings and off balance. See the splinters in both churning tub and plunger? It's no wonder poor Colley does not wish her milk in it."

The cow in question let out a loud fart in agreement, it seemed. Laughter washed over the tavern's walls.

The widow massaged behind the cow's ears, which seemed to ease her distress. "And if the captains will permit my further observation," she continued, "the Wyatt pasture adjoins our Raven Hill, so I have some knowledge of its condition. It is badly fenced, so that his cow is kept tied to a stake in the ground. She only has a circle of new spring grass to eat. I believe it is a wonder she gives any milk at all."

"You help us form a full notion of circumstances, good woman, and we thank you," Captain Worthing said, with a warmth in his voice that seemed to travel to the widow's cheeks.

The captain next called the Wyatt maid to step forward. He spoke to her gently. "As your master has not seen fit to make introductions, may I ask your name?"

The maid stood only a little taller than William English, I judged, perhaps four and a half feet. She was small-boned, adding to her child-like appearance. But her back was straight, and her red hair neatly braided around her head. "You may indeed, captain," she said in a clear voice. "It is Abigail Barrie."

"And you are in service, indentured to the Wyatt household, Abigail?"

"Aye, sir."

"How many years are left on your term, child?"

"Two years, three months and twenty-seven days, sir."

"An exact rendering! And your present age?"

"I turned fifteen years on the seventh of July last, sir."

"Again, a precise accounting, lass."

She raised her glance to both judges. "I can track important numbers, sirs."

"Aye, she defaces the walls of my barn with her scratching of days!" her master claimed.

Captain Lacey frowned. His cinnamon scent intensified. "Unless you are adding this to your list of complaints before us, it is not your time to speak sir," he said.

"Beg pardon, your honors," George Wyatt murmured, squirming in his place on the bench across from ours.

Captain Lacey nodded to his fellow judge. Captain Worthing continued. "Now, to the matter at hand, Abigail Barrie. Did you ask Charlotte Jaddore to treat your arm?"

"Aye, sirs. The very day she returned to us with her baskets of herbs from her study with her honored grandmothers. She hired me out for some cleaning duties, then visited straight after to see to my hurt. She is all kindness, our Charlotte."

"And what did she do for your injury?"

"We made a paste of balsam needles. She brought sarsaparilla bark too, so we made tea."

"I heard incantations!" her master shouted.

Captain Lacy sighed. "More accusations, Master Wyatt?"

He looked out to the back wall again, seeming to gain courage from someone in the crowd. "Aye!"

Captain Worthing leaned forward. "Then, another question for you, Abigail. What of your master's claim of this?"

"They were not incantations, sirs, they were the Mi'kmaq words for medicines. I asked Charlotte to teach me them." She closed her eyes. "Oisapegelao and gtjugaoapi." Her eyes found mine. "Is that right, Charlotte?"

I nodded. "That is exactly right."

"You have a good ear to go along with your figuring abilities, child," Captain Worthing observed. "Please allow me to be among those offering you wage employment when the term of your indenture is over."

"With pleasure, Captain," she said, with a small curtsy.

"Now, answer me this, Abigail. Was your arm sore from your efforts at this misbegotten churn?"

She cast her glance upon her master, who frowned. "I—I cannot say for sure, sir."

"Cannot or will not, for fear of a beating, lass?" Captain Lacey asked gently.

Abigail said nothing at all in response.

"None will tell me how to deal with my servants!" her master answered into her silence.

My father growled but he allowed my hand to stay him. His Vice Admiral rose, his powerful form belied by the gentle tone of his voice.

"Abigail, you are most brave to stand firm on the side of Mistress Jaddore's innocence in this matter. I urge you to feel free to speak up on your own mistreatment before this court."

"Aye, sirs. Thank you, sirs. It is not so bad." She eyed her master now. "Yet."

Her champion nodded. "Should it become so, we will listen."

His fellow judge cast a glaring look upon my accuser. "Now, to you, George Wyatt."

"I did not say witch," Famer Wyatt now maintained. "Did I once call her a witch? I only wanted her to undo her spells, honored admirals! And now I fear her father's piratical eye on me! It is cursing me forevermore!" Lightening flashed and a spring thunderclap sounded in the distance. "There, see?" he claimed now. "I am doomed by the ill wind father and daughter cast upon us here today!"

His cow bayed out a mournful cry.

Captain Worthing sent forth his own thunder. "Sit down, sir!"

His fellow judge waited for all murmurings to cease. The room becalmed, except for the distant thunder. Captain Lacey began his pronouncement. "George Wyatt. Mend your fences so that your cow need not be hobbled and have purchase of more of your meadow," he said sternly. "And, if you are in want of butter, lend your arm to the repair of this churn, and then to its working, for I suspect young Abigail's arm needs time as well as the balsam to regain its strength."

He then conferred with his fellow judge. My father kept his distance from the admirals, stroking the quill and bead earring my mother had fashioned for him long ago. The only sound that could be heard over Captains Worthing and Lacey's murmuring deliberations was the scratching of Randall Kelly's drawing pen.

Finally, standing close to the center of the tavern so all could hear, Captain Worthing spoke. "Treating a woman or child with disrespect will be judged with severe consequence whilst we are fishing admirals. They are small in number among us, yet essential to the success of this colony. Their number will be smaller still if we show them harshness or dishonor. It is our judgement that you have done both, George Wyatt. For the first you will reduce the term of indenture of Abigail Barrie by six months. For the second, you will mend your fences and free your cow of her hobble. Once her milk increases, have your maidservant deliver to Charlotte Jaddore's expanded household one quart every baking and Sabbath days for the enjoyment of the children now residing under her roof. To be subject to the careful measurement of the esteemed Abigail Barrie, of course, who will also report on the state of her harmony with her master. Directly to Captain Jaddore, who has a discerning, but never an evil eye."

My father's fingers ceased their stroking of his earring. I hoped he was listening to the voice of my mother within as he stood to finish the day's proceeding. His eyes scanned every face in the room before he spoke in a slow, measured voice.

"I have but one statement. I do not speak as an admiral, but as one among you, Martin Jaddore, captain of the *Esperance*. I will have none disparage my daughter. She has devoted herself to St. Anne, grandmother of the Christ, a woman revered by the Mi'kmaq people as well. Charlotte Jaddore has been studying the traditions of our friends who are long natives to this island. She has followed the ways of her esteemed grandmothers as well as those of the gentle and vibrant woman who was my wife. Some of you have had dealings with my inland relatives. In a week's time we will sit in judgement of a case that involves them. I have named my daughter an interpreter in these proceedings. You know that neither she nor our friends are the devils that fear paints them. St. John's, Avalon, indeed this island of Newfoundland is not part of Satan's Empire." He now met the eyes of all in the crowd, lingering only on Farmer Wyatt for a moment more before he finished. "If any of you wishes to do further battle with the phantoms of diseased minds, let your God help you, for I will not!"

His proclamation was met with a profound silence, and then cheering.

The English children enjoyed the cow's milk component of the admirals' judgement, and even more the lively company of Abby Barrie, who knew skipping rhymes and concocted wonderful puddings and sweet cakes with the milk she brought us midweek on baking day. And on her Sabbath day visit, she was even cheerful as she listened to the dreary paced singing from Mary's treasured psalm book.

Chapter 8
The Case Against the Beothuk

There was a judgement my father's able admirals had made careful preparations for while we were in Salem. It involved an accusation against the Beothuk, and so both my language skills and my father's diplomacy were needed, they assured us. They sent word by way of our friends among the Mi'kmaq to our most reclusive neighbors that a circle council had been called, which was the shape our deliberations took when a case involved our native friends.

On the day the counsel was to meet, our population swelled with inland forest dwellers, arriving in their birch canoes from various bays and inlets around. Our Salem cousins shrunk away when the Mi'kmaq entered our storerooms. Among them was Darting Badger, who was a fellow translator and bridge person with the reclusive Beothuk people. He and my father had known each other since they were boys. He and his family often looked in on me when I was wintering with my grandmothers. He was inches taller than even my father, who was almost six feet in height. He wore his half-shaved hair long and wore a fine summer linen shirt and red robe. His wife's Beothuk friend Asson had adorned both with her quillwork. She added designs from the glass trade beads that were my father's gift from faraway Venice. I was so lost in tracing their images of bears, caribou, salmon, and seals that I did not see trouble ahead.

Young Philip's bluster almost caused a rift in our alliance when he reached for one of our hunting knives as Darting Badger ruffled William's hair.

"You will not have my brother to carve to pieces!" he informed our guest.

With the swiftness of the animal he was named for, Darting Badger had the knife sailing out of William's grip and spinning. It slashed through the air and came, pointed edge down, on a wooden bowl I'd carved from a tree burl. Its lodging made the metal of the knife sing.

Mary pulled her siblings against her in a desperate huddle.

But little William escaped her hold. He planted his little feet before Darting Badger and threw his arms out. "Again!" he demanded.

Darting Badger laughed. Then he nodded toward young Philip. "These English children have a fearsome protector!" he proclaimed.

Did I see Philip smile, even as Mary's fingers tightened on his shoulder?

Our guest pulled the knife from the bowl and inspected the tip. "Well made," he judged. "I will trade for it. It will help my wife skin beaver. But I do not desire this bowl of your making, Charlotte Jaddore. It leaks."

I took it from his hands. "It now holds only a story."

"Ho!" he agreed. "Its creation is complete, then!" He laughed again. It felt like music washing over us.

* * *

As the sun reached its zenith, we gathered at the hearing circle my father presided over that day as admiral. Our whole community had gathered, including coopers, blacksmiths, wheelwrights, carpenters, and masons and their families. Only a few West Africans who had sailed out into the open waters early that morning to fish, and Mr. Fewing and a small number of his afternoon patrons at the Sea Parrot were not among us. The storehouses and shops, the flakes and vats for rendering cod liver oil were still. Gardens were untended. Pigs, cows, sheep, and ponies roamed free in our green spaces. Most of our community, it seemed, wanted to see what sort of justice would be rendered fit by my father and his admirals. And if we would add New World conflict to the hardships visited upon us by the wars in the Old.

74

The dispute centered around a grievance against people of the Beothuk, so my father had asked a group of the Beothuk's kin of the Mi'kmaq people to be their emissaries. There was some grumbling in the crowd as they entered the circle. As was the custom of our guests, we all sat on blankets on the ground, so that no one's head was higher than another's. My father and his admirals were spaced apart from each other within the circle. It was all vastly different than court proceedings that took place inside the tavern. That led to yet more grumblings which my father and his admirals ignored. Darting Badger and I took our places as translators.

James Brewster, the Master of Raven Hill, a man of about fifty, approached. Like Darting Badger, he was dressed in his feast day finery, including a full cinched, indigo-dyed coat and curls-to-the-shoulder black wig so large and full that he had his tricorn hat tucked under his arm so as not to disturb it. He was flanked by his two sons, Gideon and Samuel, dressed almost as grand as their sire. Master Brewster's new wife was not among the family group.

He stepped into the center of the circle and bowed politely to my father where he sat on the circle's eastern side. He found the vice and rear fishing admirals in the south and west parts of the circle and granted them an extra flourish of his ostrich feathered hat. He only nodded toward the northern part of the circle, where Darting Badger and I sat with the delegation of Mi'kmaq elders.

"Captains," Merchant Brewster began, "The peace was broken this winter. My sons and I were grievously misused by a band of Beothuk who made their way from the interior on Christmas Day last to burn the prime of our family's fishing stations. They made off to their savage homeland, leaving the shoreline bare except ash."

"Were any at the station when this occurred?" Vice Admiral Worthing's booming voice asked from his part of the circle.

"No, sir, it was shut down for the winter."

"Who overwinters as caretakers of supplies and properties?"

"My sons, sirs, who live above, in their own houses on Raven Hill estate."

"To your sons then: where is your evidence that this was a Beothuk raid?" asked Rear Admiral Lacey.

"Tracks, sir," Gideon Brewster, the elder of the two said.

"Aye," his brother announced, louder. "We all know the tracks of Beothuk moccasins. They led through the pass leading into their winter camp and their half-buried hovels."

"Did you follow these tracks?"

"And risk an ambush and the loss of our lives?" Gideon spoke up indignantly. "We did not!"

Sounds of consternation began among the Mi'kmaq elders.

"What evidence have you that the fire was set by the red Indians?" the rear admiral asked.

"Evidence? Evidence?" Samuel, the second born asked. "Did they not wait until a day of remembrance for Christians? Did we not give chase to the thieving scoundrels back into their woodlands?"

Mumblings and occasional shouts of "Aye! Where is justice?" rose higher. My father raised his hand. With the simple gesture, all went quiet.

He spoke for the first time since the proceedings began in his calm, French-accented English. "It is time we heard from our neighbors," he said.

Darting Badger looked to me. I nodded. He stepped forward. "Thank you for welcoming us to your council. I have come on behalf of our kin the Beothuk. They tell a different story- of three boys of the people Beothuk, fishing for eel, being drawn to a glow in the night sky. Of the shouts of an argument between two men as they tried to put out flames with their cloaks. Of these boys watching. Watching only, until the men gave up their battle with the flames and fell down. The boys heard their..." Darting Badger turned to me. "*Shewthake?*" he asked for a translation of a Beothuk word that was the sound like a grindstone. "Snoring," I whispered, and he repeated, louder. He waited for the titters to die down before he continued. "The two did not move. The Beothuk boys, they helped another one pull them toward the shore."

"What one?" my father asked.

Here Darting Badger hesitated. I touched his arm. He did not look into my eyes. "A shadow. They did not see clearly," he whispered.

"*Something sacred?*" I asked him in Mi'kmaq.

"*No, no,*" he whispered, then, louder, and in English, "Another, who they did not know. Only when all were gone," he continued, "those youth dared each other to walk back down to the fish station. Not a station—" Darting Badger leaned down to me and asked for help in translation again. "Charlotte, *possthee*?" "Place of smoke remains" I tried. He nodded, satisfied. "Remains," he said carefully. "It was the remains of the station, burned, blackened, finished. The children gathered iron nails that the fire left behind."

Grumblings started from the crowd around. Darting Badger held up his hand. "Yes. This they did. Take the iron. Their families are sorry that they took what was not theirs. They offer the burned metals' return, now that it is made into six good spearheads and twenty fishhooks. Well-made and sharp. Their grandmothers also offer five baskets, to atone for their mischief. He lifted the fishing nets covering the objects—large birch baskets decorated with porcupine quills and red ochre dye. The largest one had a rainbow design of glass beads. There was a hushed silence, for the beauty of that basket stole our breath. Asson's work, I was sure.

"The grandmothers make these offerings to restore the peace. But these boys did not set the station on fire, that was done by the men sleeping on the shore."

Silence followed the narrative.

"Captains!" both the Brewster sons shouted at once, each facing the vice and rear admirals.

"You did not reveal where you were at the time of the fire," Captain Worthing said.

Gideon lowered his head, but not his brother. "You did not ask!" Sam said.

Their resplendent father only faced mine, as he spoke in a calm, but seething voice. "Martin Jaddore. Are you going to believe us, or the admitted thieves?"

"We are going to gather more of the story," my father informed him evenly. "Mr. Kelly, would you kindly fetch us our tavernkeeper Fewing?"

Randall raised his head, handed me his sketchbook and made for the tavern on our small square.

The brothers appeared nervous. "Do you not take us at our word, sir?" Gideon huffed.

My father's even stare stopped the man's twitching. "My fellow admirals and I were not here. Nor was your father. We are wanting a full picture of the night."

His vice admiral nodded. "To picture it in our mind's eyes," he agreed.

Tavernkeeper Issac Fewing, a stout, bandy-legged man soon appeared, a cleaning cloth still draped over his shoulder. Randall took his place beside me, and retrieved his book of tinted paper and chalk once more. "This is getting interesting," he whispered at my ear. "Who is the mystery rescuer, have you an idea?"

"None."

The admirals turned their attention to the tavernkeeper, who removed his skullcap to reveal a bald head. How can I serve your honors?" he asked them. "I water down no wine!" he insisted.

The admirals turned their gaze to my father. "We seek your recollection only, sir," Vice Admiral Worthing intoned.

"At this time," Rear Admiral Lacey said, frowning.

My father sighed. "The day on which our Lord's birth is celebrated, sir, was your establishment part of that celebration, Mr. Fewing?"

"Indeed, sir. With songs and merriment, and a visit by Mummers, dressed in their animal skins, dancing as hobby horse and dragon, masks and stuffings. Even a one, a tall one, with a caribou skull set atop! Aww, now, you must not recriminate us for our world turned upside down season, sirs! It's a hard and lonely life for those wintering over...and we mean no lasting disrespect for your esteemed authority! Do not you take away—"

"We are not interested in the nature of your revelry, man," Captain Lacey assured him impatiently, "only in an accurate reckoning of the night."

"Oh? Well, then, your esteemed honors, the early night was fair and clear, like in the gospel of Luke, and much comfort and joy and luck were wished to all at the start of our season of the returning light."

"And were the men of the Brewster family among the revelers of the night?"

"Aye, sir. With the father away at sea, well, the sons were among the last to make their way home, hours later, when the fog had descended upon us."

"With wine bottles in tow?" Captain Lacey asked.

"Aye, sirs. And they've yet to settle their bill in full." He looked around at the suddenly grumbling crowd. "I make no complaint, your honors, I am a patient man and I know my place."

"Your duty to our community at this moment is to tell the truth," my father informed him mildly. "Were these men far into their cups?"

"I would judge so, sir. And into an argument so far that I urged them to continue it outside. It stood out amongst the general harmless merriment, you see? I thought their smoking clay pipes would set our gathered greenery boughs alight with their gesturing, I must say. It was a waxing crescent quarter moon night, to my recollection, I set them out in."

"Do you know the source of their dispute?"

"Ah, the argument could not have been kept from any within, your honors-- even among the toasts to our good health, wealth, and sovereigns of every nation under the sun and kingdoms of the air and sea besides. Their bitterness blossomed early in the night—their father's displeasure over quality of work put in by the heirs. And later the talk stemmed out and was of the father's selling off a portion of their inheritance to buy the years of indenture remaining on a serving maid and taking her to wife. They begrudged him sailing to New York to proper marry with her, you see. Aye! And herself the beauteous object of affections of many a lonely planter man the shoreside around, was she not?"

Captain Worthing sighed. "And how was the fire discovered, do you know?"

"By the traveling mummers, sir, who were making their way home after visiting around. They called the alarm and brought us by and by."

"And the Brewster brothers?"

"They were asleep. Aye. Dead to the world, and with tracks showing some good

Samaritans hauled them away from the flames and toward the water."

"You were there?"

"Oh, aye, sir. Many were there, heaving sand around, so as to keep the spread of the fire at bay."

"And you saw no sign of Indians?"

"Only Sam and Gideon, sir, who when finally roused, were no help at all."

"Did they speak of Indians?"

"No sir. Of their own troubles, they spoke. And of them seeing the giant stag with red eyes, the harbinger of disaster."

"Giant stag?"

"Aye sir, which we took to be the mummer with the stag head, and paid him little mind."

"What else did they say, Mr. Fewing?"

He scratched the few hairs on top of his head. "Mumblings, except for Gideon's 'We'll catch the very hell now, brother.' I remember that."

The listeners grew so loud in their reaction then that the vice admiral had to remove his shoe and bang it down to quiet them.

After listening was restored, my father spoke. "You hear many a dispute, in your choice of making your living, do you not, Mr. Fewing?"

"Aye! Dispositions cast high flames... fair and foul both within walls of the Sea Parrot, sir."

"And did you hear any centering around Indian raids in the wintering over season past, sir?"

"Not a one. Not of Mi'kmaq or Beothuk scallywags either one, your vaulted honor. Much more talk was of the late aggravations of our own navy against the French Shore, truth be told, and the foolishness of that. What I hear is fear of what the French forces might do to St. John's in answer, to spoil our way of life here."

"But there is precedent of burnings and thievery."

"In the old days, before the planters wintered over, before our Mi'kmaq allies stood as go-between with their kin, as Darting Badger and your own most worthy daughter do now, Captain."

My father turned to Darting Badger, who was standing among the gifts of the Beothuk, as still as the tavern keeper was loquacious. "How do you find these conflicting stories?" Papa asked him.

Darting Bader looked to me. Whispering, he asked if he should stand beside my father. I nodded. He took a few slow steps, turned to face our assembly, then began in a slow, clear voice. "We of the Mi'kmaq are your friends. Long ago we became Christians. Our religion sits easily with our old ways, another arrow in our quiver. We also honor the truth. Can the truth of that night of the burning be known? The Beothuk believe their children, Master

Brewster believes his." He swept the air beside the iron fishing spear tops, hooks, and the beautiful baskets. "Here before you are the peace offerings of the young ones and their grandmothers. My heart tells me they should be honored and accepted."

He returned, sat beside me and asked in the Mi'kmaq language, *"Is it wise to speak from the heart to these people?"*

"Not always. But today, I think, yes." I answered.

My father consulted with his fellow judges. He then called the murmuring crowd back to order. "I thank all who gave testimony," he began. "Please bring forth the scale, Admiral," he addressed Captain Worthing formally.

His fellow captain lifted high the balancing scale that my father once told me was in the style revered by the ancient Greeks-- a simple dishes and chain design. He then asked Darting Badger to place on one side the fishhooks and spear head offerings of the Beothuk.

He then called me. "Charlotte, would you please take this box containing nails from our stores and add them, one at a time, to the other side of the scale?"

This I did, to an enthralled audience. I was glad my father had not asked me to wear a blindfold to complete my role as Lady Justice. Finally, the scales tipped even and I stood back.

My father walked to a place beside me. "I thank Darting Badger for his eloquence and wisdom," he said. "We agree with him that the truth cannot be known."

He took a deep breath before his pronouncement. "This is our judgement. From my storehouse I will donate these nails needed for the Brewster family to rebuild their fishing station. They will accept them and the gifts Darting Badger has brought." He took a deep breath before he continued. "And they will demonstrate their own good faith by giving the families of the boys who saved them from the flames two mated pigs."

"Two pigs!" burst forth from all three Brewster men.

"To seal this agreement between you and for the sake of peace in this community. Is this settlement agreed upon?"

"Might we consult--" the master of Raven Hill began.

"No. Decide. Now." My father was out of his famous patience.

With his sons continuing to bicker at his side, Master Brewster raised a steady gaze to my father's eyes. "We agree," he said.

I leaned close to my father's ear. "The people were with you," I whispered.

"Perhaps," he said. "And we gave them good entertainment in our justice seeking. But, Charlotte, know this: we have also made enemies this day."

Still at my side, Darting Badger nodded his agreement.

Chapter 9
Death Comes to Avalon

Cousin Mary was most at ease in my food and herb garden, I think, though she had strong feelings about its tending.

"These are pitiful beginnings."

"We are in a colder place than yours. The seasons are later."

She looked to the sky. "I cannot imagine any place colder than where I live."

I laughed. "Come with us next time I climb the cliffs with the boys. See the ice giants that remain at sea. They may convince you."

"I am at prayer when you lure my brothers away."

I tamped down any objection to her wording with a smile. "Can we not pray anywhere, cousin?"

She considered. "Do you take your bible to the cliffs? Do you read scripture?"

Her questions felt like the verbal sparring that Papa and I sometimes did, but with darker intent. "We breathe in wonder at creation," I offered.

"Coveted wonder? Do you want for its possession, Cousin Charlotte?"

"Possession? Who can possess the sky? The sea? The earth?"

She hesitated, then a small smile of conviction lit upon her face. "It is from high cliffs that the devil tempted Jesus, promising him the world around."

Well, she had me stumped then. I never understood that passage, or devils, or temptations. Why did not both Jesus and Satan admire the beauty spread out before them from their mountaintop? "Well, best to harken to the world under our feet now, or these beans will not be planted." I pushed my pole into the sun-softened ground. "Perhaps you will not have to endure a single winter here. Perhaps all will be well in Salem before then."

Mary became quiet after that, and I feared I had been unkind, wishing her away from my home, my seasons with my father and my bustling, boisterous community ready to welcome the return of summer and its bounties of land and sea.

But when we'd finished planting the hills of fast-growing Gaspe corn, beans and squash seeds, she spoke quietly. "I should like to come with you and my brothers for your next sunrise walk. I will bring my prayer book and sing a psalm of thanksgiving for deliverance from our troubles to this place."

"You would be most welcome among us," I said, with perhaps more enthusiasm than I felt.

Salem's troubles had already infected our beloved island. I knew that from the whisperings about the strangeness of our cousins, delivered forth from the land of witches. And from my own trial, as comical as it may have seemed to all but my father. Then of course came the Brewster family fire and complaint against the Beothuk, and the looks of resentment we'd been getting over the way it was decided.

Randall had tried to make light of the lingering animosity. "Perhaps if your father had not made the Brewsters give up the pigs, all would be well," he quipped.

I had guessed why. "The Beothuk grow hungrier as they are pushed inland by the settlers, away from their fishing coves. My father fears for them for they no longer risk coming to the shore very often. Raising pigs for food might help them get through the winters."

He shrugged. "Or the poor squealers will be stomped to death by the caribou herds."

Salem's fears visited us in the same way sicknesses came to Avalon. In mounting waves that threatened to engulf us all.

They began a new, more deadly phase on the day my young cousins and I trudged to our sunrise watch on a foggy morning in June. Mary opened her book to find a suitable Psalm. I caught young Philip smile as she began to sing, "O give thanks unto the

Lord; for he is good: because his mercy endureth forever."

He leaned close to my ear as I shifted little William to my hip. "Number one-eighteen," Philip informed me. "Well, that one's got but twenty-nine lines at least."

He bellowed out the words with their doleful tune alongside his sister. By the time they'd reached "I called upon the Lord in distress: the Lord answered me, and set me in a large place," the sudden anguished notes of the golden-headed gannets alerted us that all was not well. As the ever-stronger summer sun burned through, Philip pointed below us to the shoreline.

"Is that man asleep, Charlotte?" he asked.

William and I looked over the edge. The splayed figure below did indeed appear to be in repose in the sand. Except for the mis-jointed arm and leg that pointed to a more sinister interpretation of his state.

"Perhaps," I said quietly.

"We'd best wake him, before the tide carries him out to sea. Or the gulls carry him off. Look how they gather, pecking at his neck. He does not awaken! Why does he not fight them off, Charlotte?"

I touched the medicine pouch hanging from woven ribbons against my left hip. The teachings of my grandmothers in their gentle, patient voices entered my mind through my fingertips. In my pouch was ka'qaqujuinmusi—bone medicine, to help the body heal fractures, and sweet myrtle to chew on to relieve pain. But I knew, as I felt the shock, the affliction of his last moments still riding in the air around us, the being below us was no longer in pain, no longer in need of anything in my pouch.

William, in my arms, the toddling babe closer to the crossroads of life than the rest of us, knew it too. I felt the palm of his soft little hand press my cheek, pulling me out of the imagined agony of the fallen person's landing and back into the vibrant, living world, which was suddenly too beautiful. "Thank you, Will," I whispered, before handing him to his sister.

"Mary, I will go down. Please take that path and return to our house and fetch my father."

"I can run faster than Mary with William as her burden, cousin," Philip said brightly. "Shall I go ahead of them?"

"Yes," I agreed. "That would be a great help."

I watched them only a moment before I wound my way down the cliff's side to wave the birds away from the body of the dead man.

Despite the fog lifting and the sun of a bright day burning through, I felt a chill to my bones as I stood guard over the well-dressed corpse. A fellow merchant, or well-landed planter, I felt sure, as I felt for signs of life at his wrist. There were none. He was bewigged, though its curls were askew after the gulls had pecked at the tender parts of the neck. The corpse was faced down, or they would have pecked out his eyes first. A small mercy.

It was a lonely vigil. My presence was enough to keep the seabirds at bay. I stood praying for the repose of the soul of the person whose fingers still grasped for purchase in the air even as they ground into the sand of his final landing.

I welcomed the sound of my father's familiar footfalls, followed by the more halting ones of Randall Kelly and his walking stick.

After a quick embrace and a kiss to my forehead, Papa and Randall gently turned the figure to his left side to reveal the anguished face of James Brewster, the master of Raven Hill.

"God rest his soul," Randall murmured, touching his own forehead and then to a place over his heart. He looked up to my father. "A fall?"

"After a struggle, mayhap," Papa said, indicating a gash across the man's forehead, the patch of red dirt ground into his coat's back, and the bloodied, crushed fingers of his right hand.

Randall reached between two of those fingers. He held up a small, filigreed silver button, released from their death grasp.

"Holy Mother of Mary," I intoned our beloved St. Anne, "Did someone send Master Brewster to his death?"

My father's eyes were sad. "It appears so, *ma cher,*" he said.

Chapter 10
Condolences

Randall covered the body with his cloak and walked toward the town, while my father and I climbed up to Raven Hill.

The household was bustling with early morning activity around the mansion house. Lumbermen were already sawing trunks into timber. Raven Hill's housekeeper, the estimable Widow Gavin, walked toward the main house with a basket of eggs at her hip. She smiled at our approach.

"Well met, Captain Jaddore and daughter. My mistress will be happy for your company."

"I fear not, good lady," my father said, removing his hat.

I reached for her hand. "Please stay," I entreated her, for Mistress Brewster was the second of her title, and closer to my age than her husband's half century of years. Their housekeeper was a calm and sweet presence, with wisdom that far exceeded my own.

Widow Gavin sat quietly beside her mistress as we delivered the news of her husband's demise. Rose Brewster wore a day gown, her fair hair braided but as yet unpinned. She was uncommon tall, slender and paler than I'd remembered before I'd left for my winter camp among my grandmothers. I was still not used to her being Mistress of Raven Hill at all, for she'd been Rose Hardy, who'd come over with her brother on the *Esperance*, two Atlantic crossings past.

Rose looked down at her folded hands and did not speak for a long time. Finally, she raised her head and focused on my father's eyes. "Did he suffer, Captain?"

"I think not. His neck was broken in the fall."

My father had seen enough falls from the mast to know that, I surmised.

Rose squeezed the widow's hand. "That is a mercy, aye?"

"Indeed, Madame," My father agreed.

"My brother suffered so." Rose turned to me. "Remember I told you of his starving to breathe, Charlotte?"

"I do."

The lost look in her eyes pierced my soul. "Daughter, sister, wife. Who am I now?" she asked the air before her.

"Widow, sweetling," Mrs. Gavin said gently. "Like me. Like too many women, old and young, on this seafaring island. And you will be a mother, with a lovely child to ease your sorrows, come Fall."

I thought there was something different about the look of Rose.

"Would you like to lie down awhile?" the housekeeper asked now.

"Oh, no." She stood. "I need air, and a walk. So that I might think. Will you please excuse us, Mrs. Gavin, Captain Jaddore? May I take your arm, Charlotte?"

So we left my father with Mrs. Gavin to discuss alerting the dead man's grown sons, and see to arrangements for gathering up the body and laying the deceased to rest.

The new widow directed our walk to the edges of her estate, where trails led to beautiful vistas of the sea gleaming in the morning sun.

"I love this spot. And watching the birds. Will he make me leave here?"

"Who?"

"Gideon. Is the house and land all his now?"

"Rose. This is your home. Your husband's son would not—"

"I think he would turn me out if he could. And Sam will follow his brother like a trained dog, although he is the cleverer of the two. Can they send me into the wilderness? And Mrs. Gavin, will they reward her kindness to me with eviction as well?"

"I know not," I admitted.

"Remember our talks when we were young, Charlotte? I wanted to be mistress of this grand mansion house. And he was so gentle and considerate in his courting. I thought I would grow more fond of him, because he was so kind, after my brother and his protection in this world of men was lost to me. Should I have refused his suit? Should I have served out my indenture? Was I not brave enough, Charlotte?"

"You are very brave indeed," I tried to assure her. "You crossed an ocean."

"Only because I heard that you did too. Peter said he knew if I was found out to be a female among the hired-on crew that Captain Jaddore would not string me up, or toss me overboard, because of the tales that his own daughter sometimes dressed as a shipmate. So, we hatched our plot. Peter would not have to leave me behind to starve, or sell my body, you see? It was because of you."

"I did not know I played that part in your story."

She turned from the sea and faced me, taking my arms in her hands. Strong hands, with long fingers. "I am sorry for our falling out since my marriage, Charlotte. I do not excuse myself, but this family had a part in it. They turned, soon after the ceremony in New York." She released me and turned back to the sea. "It was a grand time, full of lovely walks and visiting around and gifts. The Dutch are so splendid with their gifts and sweet things to eat. And I learned to dance the minuet and allemandes and how to set table and speak more properly. My teachers were so kind and patient. They called me my husband's long-stemmed rose, imagine. It was like heaven, was New York Island. I could not wait to tell you all about it. But then we returned. To this island. The menfolk, they said if I wanted to be the mistress of this estate, I should obey my elders, and not associate with or even admire a woman of the wild- that being you- a red Indian, who her father neglects, when he is not indulging to a scandalous degree."

I felt a flare of anger and was ashamed of it in front of this new widow, whose troubles were so much greater than my own. And it was good to have reaffirmed that some of this island would always see me as related to my mother's people only, and therefore a stranger, even an enemy, because many among the Mi'kmaq were allies of the French and we were at war.

Rose continued, as she looked far out to sea. "I was not content as a bondswoman, indentured to a family almost as kind as I remember my own. And I was so lost after Peter died. He died when you were with your grandmothers, so I was even angry with you for not being here. Foolish." Her glance darted about the whitecaps of the waves below us. "I have done so many foolish things. And now I must protect this child, who is innocent of all my folly."

"You have friends, Rose," I said softly. "You are not alone."

"Am I not? Will you forgive my coldness toward you, Charlotte?"

"Of course."

"And will you help me," she looked to her middle, "when my time comes?"

"Yes. Your request honors me." I gave her the formal answer I'd been taught by my grandmothers, for when a child-filled woman asked for attendance at her birth. I had attended three births in the company of my grandmothers thus far and treasured them as holy times.

Rose smiled brightly, but there was a strange glitter in her light eyes. "And Mrs. Gavin tells me you have children of your own now!"

"Cousins. Who are visiting, amidst some family distress in Massachusetts Bay Colony. They were with me this morning, when we," I faltered, "when we discovered—"

"Oh, how distressing for them!"

"They only saw from the cliffs, from afar. I sent them home for help."

"Thank you. That was a mercy. I should like to call upon you and your children, now I am a widow and not under a man's dominion. I hope I am blessed with a daughter. I must be blessed with a daughter." She glanced back up in the direction of the house. "Perhaps this family will leave us in peace, then. Might I call on you, Charlotte?"

"Yes. Of course."

"Perhaps you might be my guiding light again. Now that I am rid of him."

Chapter 11
Doubts

"Do you not think it strange, Randall?" I asked my friend later, once Mrs. Gavin led her young mistress inside for her ginger tea and a fortifying breakfast. "That Rose did not speak of her husband, still lying with his neck broken, on the shore? Or ask any circumstances of the death? Or shed a tear?"

"People show their grief in many ways, Sprite," he assured quietly, with the gift of one of his childhood names for me. "And Rose was being practical, in her circumstances, surrounded as she is up there by her husband's sons. Neither is a credit to the community around, and they are often at war with each other, over the land and those decimated fishing stations granted them by their father."

"Will they be strong enough to remove Rose and Mrs. Gavin from their home?"

"That will be determined by the conditions of Master Brewster's will."

"Did he leave a will?"

"He did indeed, written at the end of March when you were still looking for skunk cabbage with your grandmothers."

My friend could make me smile even at difficult times. "Do you know everything, Randall Kelly?"

"Far from it. But I have a curiosity that will not be sated. And I am a crier, a careful, respectful one, who does not ring out rumor or speculation, only facts. Incomplete things, facts. But they can help to illuminate minds and hearts."

My father approached. "Like who may have wanted to shove Merchant Brewster over that cliff?" he asked.

I took hold of his arm. "Papa, do you think it possible?"

"I do. But other possibilities exist."

Randall frowned. "With those crushed fingers? He was clinging to the edge, Captain. And he came away with this."

He held up the silver button, its fastening strands of metallic thread still clinging to it.

"Does it match any on his own attire?" my father asked.

"No. His were all intact. It is small, not for outerwear like a coat or cape. Perhaps it is decorative, attached to waistcoat or breeches. Or gown. They receive less wear and are more firmly attached. A strong determination pulled this loose from his killer, I think.

My father grunted. "Mayhap. We must examine the final hours of Master Brewster." He ran his hand through his hair. "As my haste to see my darling daughter has made me this year's magistrate, I have chief responsibility of finding the truth of this death."

"Murder is a capital crime," Randall reminded Papa. "A suspect needs must be sent to England for trial."

"That is why we must be sure of how Master Brewster met his violent end. And that we are firm in the belief that we have his murderer to send to the English courts, and not someone innocent. This is not Salem. But God help us all. The hunt is on."

"Who are the hunters to be, Captain?" Randall wanted to know.

"Good questions, always, out of you, darling boy. Think on it, and answer that yourselves, both of you," my father invited me into their circle. "Charlotte? Have you thoughts, my wise bridge person daughter?"

"Must we act as if ours is a community with a murderer in its midst?"

"Aye, unless a seabird plucked the flesh off those knuckles," Randall observed. "Possible. Not probable. Are we the truth hunters, then, Captain? Should discovering the circumstances of Master Brewster's demise be kept to we three only?"

My father frowned. "I think not. There will be speculation as it is. Perhaps it is best to enlist the aid of my rear and vice admirals as well."

"Unless either has reason to wish for James Brewster's death." Randall voiced a consideration of which I had not thought.

My father shook his head. "After much time in the company of these captains, both at our common ports-of-call, and here, I have found them honest and fair. Except for some sweetness Captain Worthing seems to be developing toward the Widow Gavin, they are not connected to Master Brewster's household. Might we agree to voice our concerns to him and Captain Lacey and enlist their help in our efforts?"

Randall smiled with half his mouth. "And what of your own recent court scenes with the Brewster family, sir? And your defense of the Beothuk lads and their mischief?"

"Yes, well, that cannot be helped. As you say, I am already embroiled, as is my translator daughter."

Randell crossed his arms before his chest and regarded us sternly. "Still, to serve the Lady Justice that Charlotte impersonated, I'll make sure to give you both a proper sit down before me for your testimony," he said.

We all laughed. We needed to laugh.

Chapter 12
In Mourning

And so, our efforts to reconstruct the time leading up to James Brewster's death began. Papa and his fellow admirals began by calling upon the mourning family. The young widow hosted us under the watchful eye and guidance of Widow Gavin and her tray of rum raisin cakes. Randal served as scribe there in the small counting room of Ravenhall's stone mansion house.

As my Salem cousins and I were first to spy the body, I was asked the first questions as I sat in a fine turned chair before my father, his admirals, and Randall, who took his place on a more rough-hewn wooden kitchen bench.

Captain Lacey began. "How was Master Brewster dressed, Charlotte? In his bedclothes?"

"No sir. Bewigged and in full coat with braided trim."

"Ah. And did you search for signs of life?"

"I shooed the gulls away, then felt for a pulsing at his wrist, sir."

"And found--?"

"A cold stiffness, sir. Life had left some time before, I thought."

"Did you turn him over?" Captain Worthing asked now.

"No, sir. I waited for my father and kept the birds away."

Papa's vice and rear admirals then nodded in his direction. Their few questions came to an end.

I realized then that none of us were experienced in routing out a murderer.

My father raised his voice for the first time. "Thank you, Charlotte," he said. "If my fellows do not object, I would ask my daughter to remain in attendance, to ease the sensibilities of our female witnesses, and alert the men that we value the testimonies of all."

Captain Lacey nodded his assent, and Captain Worthing added a smile of reassurance in my direction.

"Good. Please ask Mrs. Brewster to join us now, Charlotte."

I summoned Rose into the room, then took a seat where Randall left space for me on his bench.

"Your father says we are to watch for the things they do not say, but show, little sister," he said softly. I looked down from his shoulder and saw he was doing just that, with quick sketches in the margins of his paper. I did not have my friend's gift for portraiture, so I was determined to watch like an eagle and listen with the ears of a deer.

Rose's long form fit her husband's fine chair better than mine did, but she still seemed lost in the dark, mahogany paneled room that smelled of ink, smoke, and rum.

All eyes were on the young widow as her questioning began with my father's gentle voice. "Was your husband at home the night before he was discovered on the shore, Mrs. Brewster?"

"Yes, sir. We had hosted Captain Dunbar for the evening."

"Indeed? And in formal dress?"

"Yes. My husband enjoyed formality, on occasion."

"And what was this occasion?"

"We dined with our neighbor for the purpose of a discussion centered around shipbuilding."

"Were Samuel and Gideon also in attendance?"

"They were, as Captain Dunbar also sought their aid in constructing his mouth of the harbor fortifications, and to use their bequeathed land."

Captain Lacy leaned forward. "Use, Madame?"

"Aye, sir. Inland stands of oak and birch trees."

"Shipbuilding," my father surmised.

"Aye. To provide for the fishing boats and whalers. Close by and on the Grand Banks."

How far inland is it for this timbering of the trees? To the lands of the Beothuk, the Mi'kmaq people?"

"I believe so, sir."

"And what were the Brewster men's reactions to his proposals?"

"Oh, the sons liked the idea of the pursuit. They sought a partnership in the venture. They complained about the dangers on the high seas, and the trouble of mounting fishing areas every year, and the rush to find the best stations as the ships came each spring. Better to supply the ships and fishing boats- in their minds."

"And in their father's as well?"

"Less so. Fishing is...was," she corrected herself, "a prosperous pursuit of thirty years for him. He acknowledged the catches are depleting, and the political dangers in wartime. But he worried about Beothuk and Mi'kmaq raids on unprotected tree harvesters inland."

This was a Rose I did not know—not the beautiful jewel paraded on the arm of her husband since their marriage, but someone with an understanding of her family's holdings, pursuits, and commerce.

Captain Worthing then asked an interesting question, to my mind: "Did your husband seek your guidance in this proposed venture with Captain Dunbar?"

There was a pause. Rose looked at her hands. Her thumbs twitched. "Not after I spoke up for the trees."

"For the trees, Madame?"

"Yes sir. I told Captain Dunbar that I loved the trees, their shade and shelter."

"Ah," he said gently. "And the response?"

"He laughed and asked my husband if he was so enamored of me that he would be guided by my whims."

"And your husband's response to that?"

"He sent me to bed, sir."

"I see. And you obeyed him."

A faint blush spread to her neck. "Of course. I was abed until morning."

"Did nothing disturb your sleep? Voices raised? Malcontent?" This was Captain Lacey's question.

"No sir," she replied, raising her gaze to all three of her questioners. "But I am an uncommon sound sleeper."

As Rose left, I looked down at Randall's sketch of her. He'd captured not only her beauty, but also her quiet strength, as well as the new softness of both form and features. And he was thinking hard about her testimony. I could tell from the tapping of the metal tipped bone stylus he used for sketching and writing.

It was Widow Gavin's turn in the chair next.

"I was in the warming kitchen with my knitting, standing by whilst my mistress was entertaining her guests," she testified.

"And when she retired from the room?"

"I followed to help her."

"And did you return downstairs?"

"Only to see if the master needed anything more of me."

"Did he?"

"Only to decant Madeira from our cellar pipe. I did that and then left the men to their business."

"And where do you take your rest, good lady?"

"In a room above the kitchen sir, as befits my duties as housekeeper."

"Did you hear anything from below? Arguments? Anything disturbing?"

"I do not eavesdrop on my betters, sir."

"Of course. But your hearing might have noticed tones of displeasure or argument."

"Men can be loud."

"And were these men below you loud?"

"Aye, sir."

"And did the house become quiet again?"

"I could not say, sir. As I fell into my slumbers to its lullaby."

In his quick portrait, Randall captured both Mrs. Gavin's world weariness and her humor.

The questioning chair carried the men differently. It was not so much their size- the brothers were both of average height. Sam carried a bit more weight than Gideon, but neither could be termed portly. It was rather how the men held themselves in the chair— taking up its entire dimensions, from upright shoulders to knees which posted themselves squarely at its seat corners. Gideon had a slight slouch, which made the chair more of a companion when he took up its space.

He was the first of the brothers in the chair. "I have my own holding and its business to attend to," he began before a single question from the admirals. "Will this take long?"

"Not long, sir," Captain Lacey assured him. "And we thank you for your attendance. We are trying to establish when and how your father came to his death."

"The wind was high. He lost his way in the dark, the fog…"

"We understand there was a family meeting with Captain Dunbar at Raven Hill that night."

"There was. Always scheming, is Captain Dunbar."

"Did his latest timbering scheme interest you?"

He looked surprised before his mouth formed a hard line. "What did she say of it? Why did you question the women first?"

My father spoke now. "Our methods are not for you to judge, sir."

"Of course, of course," he said with a wave of his hand that seemed studied in its indifference, it seemed to me. "What was your question, sirs?"

Captain Lacey resumed. "What was your interest in the timbering?"

"I was willing to listen. That was the extent of my interest."

Captain Worthing leaned forward. "Were all of you so willing?" he asked.

"My father was less so."

"So we are given to understand."

"From whom? His wife, who wishes to stroll about her parkland forest, manicured to cushion her dainty feet? What nonsense!"

Silence reigned for a moment. Even Randall's stylus ceased its scratching. Captain Worthing bore a slight smile before his next question. "Do you think your stepmother frivolous?"

"Coddled. By my besotted father. But that is all ended for her."

"How so, sir? Has your father left a will?"

His eyes darted about the small confines of the room. "I suppose. It matters not."

"Why, sir? Has he not already provided for yourself and your brother as his heirs?"

"It matters not, I say. My brother and I, we are heirs to what remains."

"Hmmm," I heard Randall murmur beside me as the first Brewster brother was dismissed. Our view of the last night of Master Brewster's life was gaining ever sharpening perspective, like a prismed stone being polished.

Samuel was less harsh on Rose when it was his turn on the chair.

"I would never agree to turn her out," he insisted. "We are a family. But Gideon is right, she cannot have control of Raven Hill."

"Many widows run estates quite nicely," my father observed mildly.

"Widows of means and stature. This is a servant girl."

"A former servant," Captain Worthing reminded him.

"Yes, yes of course. Who is young and needs protection. And care. I am not a heartless man, captains. I will take her on if Gideon has lost his interest in her."

"Take her on?"

"Marry her. Care for her, and Raven Hill both."

"Has the lady yet learned of your intentions?"

"I – well, no. I have formulated the notion here, now." He blinked twice. "I must wait, must I not?" A sudden indignation entered his voice. "She is in mourning, sir!"

Randall leaned closer, sighing. "I thought he was the more clever brother," he whispered in my ear.

Finally, we had the last of those who spent Master Brewster's final hours with him before us. Windswept and handsome, Captain Dunbar came out of the quenching spring rain. He looked as well suited as ever in Randall's quick portrait, not even removing his fine leather gloves. Our artist captured how he habitually rested his palm on his sword hilt.

"Well met, all," his voice filled the room. "I beg forgiveness for my late arrival. Two more orders taken for shallops. Both

Spanish and French Basque whaler men require them of me. First whaling season is upon us, and a bountiful one, God-willing!" He bowed toward Randall and me, "Crier, Mistress Jaddore," he acknowledged before presenting his back to his manservant for the removal of his cape. Primus quickly left the room for the warming kitchen, his master's soaked garment over his arm. He ignored the rain dripping from his own hair.

Captain Dunbar's bow went deeper before my father and his admirals. "Gentlemen. How may I be of service?"

My father sat back as he had with the Brewster brothers. He left any cordial reception to his admirals I observed. "If you'll take that chair, we require your account of the night Master Brewster met his end," Captain Lacy began.

"I passed his sons on the way here. "You need a more coherent account of the evening, I take it?"

"Why is that, sir?"

"Both may have faulty memories."

"Due to--?"

"Their over-indulgence in spirits as we dined together."

"No one has mentioned this."

"No? Well, the family and their servants are loyal, I will credit them for that. Admirable trait, loyalty."

My father spoke for the first time. "May we have your impressions of the evening's events, sir?"

"Of course, Martin. As you know, I am seeking sources of ship-building, so that my estate will be worthy of my honored countess betrothed's presence on these shores. She rivals our late esteemed Lady Sara Kirke in her family connections and beauty of form, face, and soul."

My father only grunted.

"Aye," it was left to Captain Worthing to reply. "We are all looking forward with the greatest of pleasure toward making the acquaintance of the countess Amelia."

"And you shall! But I wish her to be pleased and proud of our holdings in the New World, in Avalon. A fine house is required, and all the comforts she enjoys at her holdings in Bermuda, and Norfolk. I thought a harvest of standing oak for stout whalers might be a profitable possibility. But I'm afraid internal disputes among the Brewster family took precedence over my seeking to purchase or lease their wooded and unimproved acreage."

"What disputes?"

"Over being removed from the main house, over the quality of land their father had bequeathed them, over his power about their right to do with their land as they pleased. I found myself attempting to make peace among them, gentlemen. I then realized my cause would only add to their disharmony. This is the last thing I would want to do—we are neighbors. So I withdrew my offer, and wished them well in settling their internal family dispute. There are other places to go for my timber needs."

"I understand the mistress of Raven Hill also held objections to your scheme."

"That poor child? A lamb among wolves, I fear. Her whims were quickly dismissed, and she was sent to bed without her supper for even speaking them."

"And when did you take your leave?"

"Oh, soon after our repast."

"And you returned directly to your home?"

"I did. My own more modest hearth was a welcome respite from the wind and fog outside and the disharmony within the Brewster household."

Randall's stylus began tapping at his depiction of the captain's gloves in his sketch. "I think the lady doth protest too much," he quoted Shakespeare quietly.

As our artist scribe was packing away his papers, my father rested a hand on his arm and called us all to attention. "We neglected to question a witness to the evening's events," he said.

"Who?" his vice admiral asked.

"Primus."

"No one mentioned Primus being there," I realized. "Not even his master."

"*Exactement*. But how have we all failed to notice?" he asked. "Captain Dunbar goes nowhere without his manservant."

Captain Lacey frowned. "This is true, of course. But, Martin, can we expect to achieve any useful information from Primus? Even a detail? He is a servant. You heard how prickly even Mrs. Gavin became under our scrutiny."

Randall nodded. "Servants have much to lose when under the watchful eye of their masters."

"This is true," my father agreed with his advisors. "Mayhap we should try getting the perspective in a more informal setting, yes?"

Captain Lacey settled his hat on over his russet curls. "Informal? But Captain Jaddore, may I inform you that this is an official inquest, being duly ascribed by our artist?"

"Precisely. And servants speak more freely away from official settings. Randall?"

"Aye, Captain?"

"Do you feel a bout of fishing for caplin in Manley's Cove coming on?"

He shrugged. "If you say so."

Chapter 13
At Manley's Cove

Capelin spawn in shallow warm water, and so Manley's Cove is a good place to find them. Capelin is a bait fish, small and caught in nets. The cod men pay handsomely for them, and stock their boats. Manley's Cove is a small bay, bounded by stands of spruce, fir, birch and pine. But it is a far walk from our settlement, and so frequented by only those brave enough to face a confrontation with a band of Beothuk who might appear out of the woodland around the cove.

Brave enough or related enough.

"I'm counting on you," a hesitant Randall admitted as we hoisted our nets over our shoulders.

Sure enough, as we rounded the last bend, there was Primus, sitting on his fine coat and looking relaxed, away from his master's imposing shadow. But he was not fishing. And he was not alone.

I recognized the woman beside him, first as Beothuk from the red oche decorations on her body and nearby birch-clad canoe. She was Asson, one of the basket makers who visited my great-grandmother Demas's camp over the winter to hear her stories and learn her craft. My grandmother gave Asson the most of her precious supply of my father's trade glass beads, because she was so skilled. The trial's peace offering of the basket with the rainbow was of Asson's design, I felt sure. She was a favorite of Grandmother Demas. Asson always listened to stories with deer ears, my grandmother once complimented her.

Asson had her deer ears on now, as she gave Primus her rapt attention.

"What is he saying?" Randall whispered at my ear.

"The dancing...of my island...is like yours," I translated from Primus' halting Beothuk.

Asson nodded eagerly. "*Oomdzech, Woodch,*" she said.

"What's going on, Charlotte?" Randall asked softly.

"She is encouraging him in his language skills. She is saying 'good, Blackbird.'"

"Blackbird?"

"Yes. I think that is her name for him."

We watched in silence, charmed by the warmth between the two. Asson took up a garment from her basket and began sewing as they continued their conversation. This was another Primus, more like the one we used to know. His face was transformed when he smiled. And he smiled and even laughed in his deep musical base voice there in Asson's company. I could not take my eyes off them.

"Charlotte," a much softer voice beckoned me suddenly, "It is I who need your language skills at the moment.," Randall said.

"But now she says—"

"Urgently, little sister."

I turned to see him between two painted red warriors. One held a knife to his throat.

I moved very slowly, facing them, making the tsking sound of a displeased gander. "Do you not know this man?" I asked them in Beothuk. "He is honored by my grandmothers. He is Weasel."

They did not move.

"Weasel with Two Spirits," I tried.

The knife lowered slowly. The warriors stepped back. Randall lifted the net from his shoulders as an offering as he laughed uneasily. "Care to join me in a catch, lads?" he asked.

I translated. Slow smiles appeared. They dusted Randall's shoulders as they apologized.

"What are they saying now?"

"They are calling you a holy person."

He laughed. "Well, I would not go so far as that."

"The grandmothers have deemed it so. Do not argue."

"Aye, of course," he promised, now sober.

We followed the warriors down to the shore. Upon seeing us, Primus took hold of Asson's hand and put her behind him protectively. The Primus we knew was back, grim and guarded, flexing those strong arms. But Asson burst forward and embraced me like a sister in spirit. After months of my cousin Mary's aloof coolness, it brought tears to my eyes.

"I love this man, Wavewalker," she said at my ear. "Help him. Help him come to us."

We turned together to face the men. Her arm stayed hitched around my waist. The look on Primus's face eased, but something else took over his eyes. He tilted his head, as I'd remembered from when he used to tell us stories of his Bermuda childhood. "My freedom, with this woman. Mistress Jaddore. I can taste it," he said quietly.

"Well, then," came out of Randall like a nervous whistle. "Best show her your net fishing skills if you want to be feeding your children someday, man." he instructed.

Primus gave us both a long, evaluating look, before he accepted my net and headed into the water with his Beothuk companions.

Randall and I sat with Asson between us. "Will it cause a war?" Asson asked, "*Woodch* coming to us?"

"We of St. John's are already at war, officially," I translated Randall's answer, "with the French. But mayhap not distracted enough fighting each other to avoid a war with the Beothuk over a bondsman's escape."

"We must find the right time," Asson said, then, in English. She trusted him enough now to let him know she understood Randall, directly.

He gave a rueful shake of his head. "Aye, lass."

"Know you have friends," I told her.

Asson touched my hand. "Friends who can keep secrets? Even from your father?"

It was a most difficult question to answer. My father was a good man, who would admire Primus claiming his freedom with the Beothuk, I felt sure. But he was also the fishing admiral, sworn to uphold the law, with harsh punishments for what Primus was contemplating. It took a long listening to my heart before I spoke. Because what we were doing was against the laws of the English. And he and his admirals were sworn protectors of those laws.

"Yes," I finally said.

Asson looked to Randall, her dark eyes questioning. He was having a difficult time making this promise too. But he also nodded his agreement.

This was no small pact between us. It was not a conspiracy of shortened study time or indulgence of sweets from our childhoods. This was keeping something important from the knowledge of our beloved Martin Jaddore.

"You must go back with them now," Asson told her beloved when he returned with his catch.

Primus bowed his head, nodded.

She handed him the cloth she had been sewing. "And tell the horse to be gentler with you," she quipped. The shirt had its once ripped sleeve carefully mended. But its cuff was missing a button.

Chapter 14
Gathering Knowledge

We had both noticed his shirt's jagged rip, and missing button.

"Shirt buttons are usually fashioned of bone or shell," Randall insisted. "Not silver."

"Usually. But his clothing contains items once worn by his master. The shirt could have had a lace attachment with a silver button showing when it was part of the ensemble of its more illustrious owner. Should we question him on it?"

"And lose the new trust between us? I think not."

"I agree. But I hate to have our suspicions come between us."

"They already have. I have cast my net of suspicion over most of the men of this island. And a few of the women. Could Primus have murdered James Brewster at his master's bidding? With a promise of his freedom?"

"Or without it, as he plans to join Asson and the Beothuk."

"We must tread very lightly. It will not go well for Primus if he is even suspected."

"Oh, Aye," said Randall. "This button question must stay between us, little sister."

Of that we were in agreement. But I kept the adornment on the mantle above our fireplace.

Primus went about his duties as before, standing by the door of our storerooms as his master shopped for items to aid him in his latest scheme. But I could tell every time Asson's beloved had visited Manley's Cove. There was a tenderness he allowed me to see in his eyes. There was something more now too since Randall and I were proving ourselves worthy of his secret.

We looked for opportunities to speak with Primus about the night James Brewster lost his life. When he tended his master's sturdy Dartmoor pony outside our warehouse store, one such chance arose. I tried not to openly search his clothing as he stroked the mare's neck with affection, but I was happy that all the buttons I could see were fashioned of tortoise shell.

"Primus, did you attend Captain Dunbar at Raven Hill on the night of his death?"

"I did."

"Was there a great deal of drunkenness on display?"

He shrugged. "No more than usual with that lot."

"And contention? Between the brothers and their father?"

"That is well-known to all, I think. But they were united that night."

"United? Over what?"

"That my master would have none of their family land, for sale or lease. That no one outside the Brewsters would. That this was their toehold in the New World, they said. Even young mistress was with them on that. She honored the trees."

I smiled. I had missed the musical cadence of his voice. "Spoken like a Beothuk."

"Now you honor me, Mistress Jaddore," he said shyly.

"There are few to whom they give their trust," I agreed.

"You see how the Beothuk treated even me, a holy person," Randall maintained with mock affront.

"I love her," Primus said quietly, with that familiar tilt of his head.

"Yes. We know this," Randall assured him.

"And you will make them all more beautiful," I added, as his master came out the door.

"Come, come, Primus, bring the mounts around, I have quarrymen contracted to enlarge King William's Fort." He looked to Randall then. "We can make use of you, crier... all hands are welcome!"

"I have a previous appointment to craft a portrait, sir," Randall replied with a wave.

"A portrait that will burn to ash like the rest of St. John's, when the French get here, lad, mark my words!" Captain Dunbar called after him. "We must all work on fortifications!"

Randall and I were glad, I think, when the two were on their way. My father often asked about our progress of finding him at Manley's Cove. I could not always meet his eyes then. We had at last acquired the perspective of Primus on that fateful night. And now we were able to report back the discrepancies between Primus's recollections and his master's,

"What would it profit Captain Dunbar to make more of an account of drunkenness and disharmony among the family, sir?" Randall wondered.

My father sat back, tapping the arm of his oak hewn chair. "Profit? Aye, profit is a good word when placed near the character of that man. Profit is his driving force, I think. And to him, we are all placed in service to it."

"And to his fortification schemes on both sides of the harbor."

"Aye, well. Those make more sense, I fear. The English continue to provoke the sun king. We may have growing settler numbers, but the French have a highly skilled army and navy both."

We looked out over our beautiful and bustling harbor streets together. It was hard to envision it in ruin. "Well, I for one, believe Primus's story over that of his master's," Randall offered stoutly, "whether that pompous man proves himself the savior of St. John's or no."

My father smiled. "On that we agree, lad. But does Josiah Dunbar refashion his perspective on that night to make himself a hero among fools who refuse to do his bidding? In his mind he's the eternal peacemaker of all speople in the lower orders than himself and his countess, is he not? The eternal protector of our harbor with his fortification schemes?"

"That will protect their wealth, their widening schemes of influence."

"Indeed."

"Or is his reasoning more complicated?" Randall asked.

"He does not seem a complicated man to me, lad. Only a bombastic one."

My father and I had good positions to talk with many islanders in the storage rooms of our house and on shore at the fishing stations. I gained a deeper knowledge of Captains Worthing and Lacey as we met with them. My father's assessment of them held. They were fair and even-tempered men. Sailors, our seasonal fisherfolk, and planters of St. John's and beyond, were obliged to them in hearing and resolving disputes, so all were used to their questions on matters pertaining to keeping the peace in our of part of the world.

The few women in our community were largely my responsibility. I found myself accepting more invitations to knitting and net-mending circles. And my visiting around extended beyond those who sought me out for herbs and remedies. I think the womenfolk thought that my expanded Salem family was the reason I took new interest in domestic duties. Young Mary was often in my company and fit in with the women better than I did in many ways. She was happy to share both her mother's household and garden wisdom, and the tunes of her beloved psalms. Me, I confess I often wished she'd left her hymnal at home.

But in the best position of all of us was Randall, who gathered information to cry out each evening. Folks were used to his insatiable curiosity. And he had a knack for disappearing into the plank walls of the Sea Parrot tavern of an evening.

To find out more of the Brewster brothers, Randall inserted friendly questions after the two were in their cups there. He described the encounter as we met by candlelight with my father and his fellow fishing admirals.

"Neither seems to be grieving overly hard," Captain Lacey observed of their indulgences.

"Aye, sir," Randall agreed. "And they do not suspect murder, I'm thinking. 'He was a clumsy man,' says Gideon, last night. 'And our beloved sire drank too much of the wine that was supposed to be used to pay our planters.'"

"'His planters, Samuel,'" I hear elder brother say in response.

'Aye, his alone once he split us off with none of our own to manage. Because of her. He was too enamored of his wife and her news.'"

"'News?'" says, I," our crier explained, "appearing all innocent of the fact, of course."

"That was not honest, Randall," I admonished him gently.

"But it was befitting of my new weasel study as commanded by the grandmothers was it not? Brother weasel does not always walk in a straight way, Charlotte, and needs to wind around to go where he is going. To get to the larger truth, I had to wind around a smaller, more insignificant truth, you see?"

My father tried to hide his smile.

"That is an interesting interpretation," I conceded warily. "Go on."

"Well, both Brewster brothers agreed on the point of their envy, that being Mrs. Brewster's condition. 'Aye, aye! Inordinately proud he was!' says Sam, 'of the child he had started. Making him feel young again. He was just a clumsy old man, who fell.'"

'The judgement against us, brother Gideon, that adds another reason for our sire's demise, that judgement favoring the red Indians made him feel a failure, having to rebuild after the fire.'"

My father held up his hand, stopping our crier's story. "But the brothers themselves refused to help in the rebuilding," he remembered.

"So I reminded them both, Captain," Randall said. They did not dispute it, but Gideon continued defending his actions thus: 'We were making our own way, had our own people to look to. He raised us up to depend on nothing but our own wits. And he became bewitched by her.'"

That word chilled the air around me. "Bewitched? Did he say that word?" I asked.

"Aye."

"Do they know that word's added power with the news coming in from the ships out of Boston and Salem? And my father's warning to George Wyatt and his claims of my spell over him?"

"Well, not him. It was only his cow, Charlotte."

My humor did not change. "How could they say such a thing of Rose?"

He held up his hand. "'Tis why I made light of it and quickly went to the favorite subject of their grievances."

"Inheritance," Captain Worthing surmised.

"Exactly, sir," Randall confirmed. "'Cut you off?' says I. 'But your family has granted land-'"

'Family land. That we'd worked together,' Gideon claims.

'Then our father parceled it, after the fire.' The other brother takes up the grievance, 'Along with family credit. He cast us off on our own.'"

"'Ah. Have you had trouble at your fishing stations this season?'" I asked.

"'Trouble? No!' Samuel insists. 'Short of help, maybe,' Gideon amends. 'No Mi'kmaq will lend a hand, or fish for us, thanks to Captain Jaddore's too-generous ruling. And the French Basques were staying clear of us since the war started. We are late. Too late, maybe to get a good trade for the cod to Boston or the Marylanders. It's a poor grade fish besides. Might have to sell it to our thieving neighbor Dunbar to feed the slaves of Jamacia.'

"Brother Sam starts another sorry excuse for their own failures, then. To wit: 'How are we to start our own families, our own estates, with so few women that even our father stole away a serving girl from us?'"

"'Stole her away?' says I.

'Aye, Gid was paying Rose court,' says younger brother."

"'Nay, I was done with her!,' says Gideon then. 'Tall as a man, and always weeping. I let him have her, I say!'"

"Do you think that's the truth of it?" I asked Randall.

"No, little sister. Rose is a rare beauty, and strong of heart and will, despite her grief over her brother. Master Brewster snatched her away from his sons, and the family who held her indenture, both."

My father posed the next question of our crier. "Would either of the brothers be angry enough to kill their own father, do you think?"

"In a fit of rage? Mayhap, poor blighted souls that we all be. And men become different creatures under the influence of the drink. But, in my observation, though they be louder versions of themselves, they are not meaner. And when sober, the Brewster lads honored their father in their own way. They are not the most ambitious of men, but they worked hard to achieve his good will."

"And their expected inheritance," Captain Lacey speculated.

"Will Master Brewster's latest recorded wishes in that regard stand, do you think?" I asked the menfolk quietly.

"Ho, have you news, Charlotte?" Randall demanded.

I hesitated. "I have rumor."

"From?" Randall prodded, as my father began stroking his earring.

"From inside the knitting circle at Mrs. Butler's cottage, as my fingers became entangled whilst trying to add speed to my lessons at the craft."

"Is that why my new scarf has many mended ties?" Randall asked.

"I fear so, yes," I admitted.

"It is as warm and will see me through winter next. Now, what did you hear?"

"I heard that James Brewster's mansion house, the farm, and all the animals were bequeathed to Rose."

My father's fellow admirals of justice smiled. A knowing look passed between them. "There's more going on at the Butler cottage than knitting," Captain Worthing observed.

My father's fingers left his earring. "Is this true?" he demanded of his admirals.

"Forgive us," Martin," Captain Lacey took up his fellow's cause. "Samuel and Gideon Brewster took their objections of this will to us, because of your role in what they consider their humiliation over the Christmas fire judgement. We meant no disrespect of your authority."

My father nodded, looking troubled still. But not about any slight towards himself, I surmised, for he was a man who did not put his own dignity above all else. "What think you of the document?" he asked.

"It was brought to us by James Brewster himself whilst you and Charlotte were in Salem, sir. Yet..." Captain Lacey looked to his fellow.

"...It is written in a hand not his own," Captain Worthing finished for him.

"Whose, then?"

Captain Lacey looked my way now. "Yours is a fine hand, Charlotte," he said gently.

"It is not mine, sir," I maintained.

My father growled before Captain Lacey nodded. "We take you at your word, of course, Mistress. But there are not many skilled at reading and writing in all of

Avalon. We are well acquainted with Randall Kelly's way with his letters. That left you as our only conjecture, so the scribe remains a mystery."

"Well, the signature on the document is his," Captain Worthing said. "And he was standing before us when he signed, attesting that it proclaimed his wishes. These are the more important facts."

"We told him its stipulations were unusual."

"And likely to be contested," his fellow admiral continued.

"That is more standard for a widow to be granted a small stipend and a room for life in the household bequeathed to the sons."

Captain Worthing frowned. "But we all know that some sons treat the standard parts of a will more as requests than stipulations. And thereby drive the second wife out. This is how Widow Gavin, with all her accomplishments, became impoverished. How she needed to seek a place as housekeeper."

"Small wonder Rose was concerned for them both," I said quietly.

"Aye, the two are fond of each other, are they not?" Captain Worthing observed.

Captain Lacey turned to my father. "I believe our obligation is to James Brewster's final wishes, Martin. He brought the will before us himself. I, for one, harbor no doubt of his sound mind and signature. And he left the document in our care. Should we not honor it?"

Of this, all three fishing admirals reached agreement.

* * *

After Captains Worthing and Lacey had taken their leave of us, Randall and my father entered our sitting room with a request. "Have you visited your friend the young widow lately?" Papa asked me.

"Should I?"

"I think perhaps, aye."

He looked to Randall who spoke quietly. "Rumors swirl in masculine circles too, Charlotte."

"About persons with 'a fine hand' at the writing?"

"Yes. About you, connected to your father and his judgement of the Brewster family grievance, and about one other besides you, that the admirals do not yet consider."

"And?" I urged him on.

"Hearsay has it that Captain Worthing's "accomplished Widow Gavin" might be literate. That she may be the scribe of the last will of James Brewster. And that she put changing his will into his mind. Before she shoved him over that cliff."

“This is a dangerous piece of gossip for an unprotected woman, Randall.”

“It is indeed. So you’d best be over there seeking a trade for some butter.”

Chapter 15
Widow Gavin

I was off to the cliffs above St. John's the next day, bringing Philip and William with me, and leaving Mary in our upstairs chambers to enjoy her bible study in peace.

"Well met!" the widow greeted me from the barn's yard. "And you must stay until my lady is up from her napping. Come inside, I have oatcakes to share with some lovely children I see before me."

We entered her sweet and hearty smelling kitchen, where she quickly agreed to my offer of two oranges, a lemon, and a replenishment of wine for three pounds of her creamy butter.

She bade us sit at the long trestle table. Then she reached for her paddle to retrieve some delights from her bake oven for us to share.

"So, the talk is true, young Charlotte, that you are seeking help to improve your baking skills?" she said, placing plates before the boys. I did not have to worry about them waking Rose from her afternoon nap. They were soon quietly engaged in the products of Mrs. Gavin's oven and berry preserve crock.

I laughed uneasily. "My expanded household and their good appetites spur me on in my efforts," I wound around the truth, whilst thinking that I should be studying Brother Weasel alongside Randall.

"Cousin Charlotte's last pound cake was not teeth-cracking hard like the first," Philip assured our hostess, "but please instruct her on how to make these oatcakes, Missus!"

"Um!" William seconded from my lap as blackberries stained his lips.

Widow Gavin felt along the soft and chubby underside of William's chin and gave it a gentle chuck. Could a woman who did that be capable of murder? "Do not fret your burgeoning cooking skills dear Charlotte," she assured me, misinterpreting my troubled expression, no doubt. "These children are thriving in your care. And under your father's protection. Would that there were more men like him in the world. Deep blessings on Captain Jaddore."

"It has not been so in your own life, Madame?"

"Indeed not. And my situation remains precarious."

This woman deserved directness, I decided, before I lost my nerve. "Did you write Master Brewster's new will? "I asked.

She did not look surprised by my question. "After his own several attempts failed, aye. Master Brewster read well but was not a practiced writer."

Attempts that might serve her own cause now, I realized. "Do you have these failed copies?" I asked.

"I do, with the laundry. Foolscap is expensive, and I thought to bleach the paper clean."

"May I see them?"

"Whatever for, dear?"

"They may add to the legitimacy of Rose's claim on this house and animals."

"Oh. Oh, my. Of course."

She fairly flew from the room, returning with three sheets of foolscap. They were full of ink stains and blotches. Upon the first was the most content. It seemed Master Brewster's instances of his sons' lack of persistence and faulty business sense were gathered until they were eight in number in that version. They were given free range until the ink ran out. His second and third attempts were progressively shorter. The handwriting was indeed faulty. But was it from Master Brewster not being a practiced scribe? Or was it the result of haste? And what might have brought on such haste? Fear? Did the man sense his own coming doom? Did he sense violence being planned against him?

All his efforts contained an admonishment to both grown sons, reminding them that he'd already divided his estate and fishing stations and helped them with the expenses of constructing their own homes. "It is therefore my wish to bequeath—" he seemed to have difficulty attaching his q's to his u's. The ink stopped this final time with a scar of black.

"You should bring these to Captain Worthing," I advised Widow Gavin.

"Why, Charlotte?"

"I think you have a protector in him, and I believe he seeks justice in all things."

"That is not all our Captain Worthing seeks," Rose insisted from the kitchen doorway, risen from her napping, and with a smile brightening her face. "Might you take a healthful stroll with me, Charlotte?"

"We protect each other, Mrs. Gavin and I," Rose assured me as we walked along the cliffs above St. John's while that lady had the boys packing slabs of her prized butter for our St. John's Day feast baking tasks.

Rose looked a sight better than the morning we'd brought her the news of her husband's fall. She wore a gown she'd fashioned from dark blue watered French silk that Master Brewster had purchased in New York when they'd wed.

"He had me display it only when we were at a public event or when we accepted offers to dine at more wealthy men's homes. But I can wear it when I please now, can I not? And it pleases me to celebrate your visit, Charlotte."

I laughed as it billowed around her. "I only hope you do not set sail."

"Not likely with my growing belly," she observed, lifting her skirts past her ankles. "Or in these."

The boots that encased her feet were heavy, their heels crusted with mud. "Charming, no?" She laughed. "They belonged to Gideon as a child. They fit me, see?" she said. "They were his father's first courting gift. I thought them from Gid. I thought he was too shy and that his father was acting as go-between. I like the boots still. They keep me grounded in the wind. There are terrible winds up here on the bluff, Charlotte."

"Terrible?"

"Oh, aye, full of wicked whisperings and discontent. Whose? Perhaps the first Mrs. Brewster. So lonely up here she must have been, living with a loutish husband and two useless sons."

I looked down at the boots again. Did Master Brewster's demise begin as an accident? Did the wind topple him over the edge as he took an evening walk with his new wife? Did she then, on impulse, seek to end their unhappy union? Those boots. Were they heavy enough to bloody a man's fingers? To loosen his desperate grip on a cliffside?

Rose stomped just then, as if answering my wonderings. I jumped. She laughed. "I caught a mouse by the tail with them just this morning in the larder. I'll bring my carving knife next time!"

I laughed uneasily.

"Why Charlotte, whatever is the matter?" she demanded now. "You look how I used to feel each morning! Mrs. Gavin brings me crackers to chew before my head has left my pillow. It is ever so much better now."

"I am glad to hear it." Was that wooden-sounding voice mine?

"You will both be there when my time comes, will you not, Charlotte? I would like to die with two beautiful faces seeing me out of this life."

"You are young and strong. We have high hopes for both you and your babe thriving together, Rose."

"Yes," she wiped a tear off her cheek. "But one needs must always prepare for death. I might see my brother again. This consoles me."

The wind whipped up stronger and with it an echo of her word "consoles." But in a different voice, it seemed. Whose? The first Mrs. Brewster? Or Rose's beloved brother? Either way, the sound admonished me, as if knowing my thoughts. What was wrong with me? How was I suspecting two women who had endured such troubles?

Chapter 16
News From Salem

"It poisons the mind, suspecting neighbors," I observed to my father that night as we supped together.

"Aye," he agreed. "I believe I am understanding the happenings in Massachusetts Bay Colony better, now."

"Has the *Gauntlet* brought news, Papa?"

"Aye, *Petite Onde*. None of it good, except that our cousins are alive. Philip writes that he saw fit to come out of hiding and join Mary and little Susanna in their Boston prison."

"Oh, Papa."

"Their wealth and status have allowed them to avoid the squalor and rent rooms of their own in their jailer's house. But if they break their agreement, they forfeit a bond of four thousand pounds."

"Four thousand pounds? Is there so much money in all the world around?"

"Not our world of bartering and credit, to be sure! But the wider world counts in gold and silver, my love. Philip and Mary's gold, or crown credit promise at least, allows them their freedom by day, before surrendering themselves back to their quarters at night. But their trial date is set. Philip fears their return to Salem might cost them their lives."

"Why?"

"Because every trial thus far has ended in conviction. Because a young refugee of the Maine frontier wars says the spirits of Philip and Mary are afflicting her."

"Their spirits?"

"Aye, 'spectral evidence.' It is damning others, innocents who do not have Philip and Mary's wealth to keep themselves distant from that blasted Salem court."

"Is Boston far enough?"

"I fear not. The accusations have broken out of Salem into neighboring communities. Philip and Mary have many enemies, eager to divide the spoils, should they forfeit their bond and escape. His voice lowered in volume. "Or an even worse fate befalls them."

"What can we do?"

"Our cousin anticipates that question, *mon onge*. He is adamant that we provide for and protect their young namesakes and Baby William. That we all remain here at St. John's and not endanger them by our further involvement in their parents' plight. He assures us that he and Mary are not without friends and allies. He has hope in the fact that Massachusetts Bay Colony has settled its dispute with the English crown. King

William and Queen Anne have sent them a new charter and governor, Phips by name."

"A man to quell their fears?"

"It is to be hoped for. But Phips is a military hero and treasure hunter. Sharing his treasure with his sovereigns is what earned him his title, some say. I have known such men in my life. They prefer action to contemplation, war to the troublesome details of keeping the peace. As governor he seems more interested in fighting Indians on the frontier than in confronting evil as it travels among his own people. He has left the trials in the hands of his lieutenant governor and his new called-into-being court."

"So, we must see what this man and his court will decide?"

"Yes. But the captain of the *Gauntlet* has informed me that proceedings have not begun well."

"How so?"

"The hangings have begun."

"Hangings?" Mary stood in the doorway. Her face had lost its color. "Who have they hanged? Do our parents still live, cousin?"

My father put on a hale expression. "They live, they live! And they are secure, dear heart." He began rummaging through the small trunk that was left in the hold of the *Gauntlet*. "And behold. Your mama and papa have sent a package to each of their Newfoundland-residing children, imagine! Look here. Yours appears the most thick, Mary."

She ignored his offering. "Has their trial begun?"

"No. But they are away, and safe."

"I had a dream. My mother was so thin. Was she dying? Dying with a baby in her arms?"

I went to my trembling cousin then. To my astonishment, Mary welcomed my embrace. Her voice was a tortured rasp. "This place they have sent us to. It is a place of fog and shadows and wind and terrible dreams," she whispered into my shoulder.

"And family," I tried to assure her. "And love."

But dreams are powerful, so I closed my eyes so that Mary would not see the fear within.

Chapter 17
St. John's Eve

I worked the sweet bread's dough on the floured board as Mrs. Gavin had instructed. Yes, it was soft and smooth under my fingers. What a good teacher she was.

My heart was gladdened to have the summer season upon us to celebrate, along with the dear patron saint of our town. I hoped it might ease our cousins' loneliness for their home and parents' company.

"Do you celebrate the birth of Saint John in Massachusetts Bay Colony?" I asked Mary as we worked the dough. Her brothers watched with patient and happy anticipation.

But from Mary, a familiar frown. "These saints and their feast days left over from the Catholic past are not celebrated, no. We believe that we are the saints, Cousin Charlotte. For among us are the elect, called upon to follow bible principles in hope of our salvation."

"But Saint John is in the bible, is he not?"

"John the Baptist is in the bible," she corrected.

"Aye, the cousin of Jesus, and this place is named for him. We honor him." I pinched off a small piece of dough and gave it to William to roll around the board under his little palms.

"Best to keep our minds on our own means to salvation than all this honoring and celebrating. It is popery, these vaunted "saints" and their relics and shrines. Better to study the bible and the word of God."

Young Philip's hopeful gaze in my direction made me try one more reason for our feast day. "Perhaps we might see it as giving thanks for the growing season and the fullness of the light?"

Her frown deepened. "Now you make it sound like heathen sun worship."

Little William raised his face to the kitchen window's light. "I love sun!" he exclaimed.

We all laughed, even Mary. Babes were a great blessing, I thought, feeling the tender stirrings of the desire for one of my own. I hoped our smallest charge would have a sound napping time, so that I might see those eyes widen with wonder at our bonfires after dark.

I did not oblige my cousins to accompany me in our other St. John's Eve traditions that morning. Alone I visited streams to honor the River Jordan where John baptized his cousin Jesus. But when I set out in the glorious warm sun to fill my basket with St. John's wort and foxgloves, wild mushrooms, plants, and healing herbs, they were waiting at the doorway, and asked to come along. And they helped me set a table outside our door with our neighborly offerings of our freshly baked bread, cheese, and beer.

Papa was busy with the other men gathering firewood for the night's great bonfire on shore, so he left us to hosting duties. From our place behind our bountiful table, we heard Randall Kelly. He blew his shell horn as the light of our long June day ended, proclaiming:

"The light fades, the hours of good amity between neighbors is upon us! Reconcile! Make bitter enemies into friends. Every door is shadowed in green birch! Approach. Seek forgiveness, before our bonfire drives out the year's evil from all hearts!"

Mary and I had just begun slicing great hunks of sweetbread for our neighbors when a man I barely recognized as George Wyatt approached. He stopped at our table and removed his hat. Behind him were two women. One was his clever servant Abigail, whose company we had been delighting in twice weekly. Her clothing was neatly patched, and she wore a lovely woolen capelet across her shoulders. Her bearing, always forthright, now had a grace that became her even further. Beside her stood an older woman. I did not recognize her, or perhaps did not see her clearly, as she was in the farmer's shadow. She pushed him closer.

"Mistress Jaddore," he addressed me. "I come seeking forgiveness for the enmity I harbored against ye this season past."

"The judgement has been rendered, Master Wyatt," I reminded him, "and you have been in compliance with your restitution."

"That is so. Yet my hardness of heart, my suspicions against you remained. It felt, Mistress, like a curse."

The women behind him sighed, then nudged his back again. He stood aside, revealing more of her form. "Beg pardon, Madame. Mrs. Roger Attley, I present to you Charlotte Jaddore," he introduced the mystery woman.

I made a curtsy to the lady in question. So, this was the reclusive Widow Attley, of the most prosperous farm of Conception Bay? Rumor swirled about her—how she had outlived a husband and two sons lost at sea, how she then turned her back from the shoreline and companionship and dedicated herself to her farm. How she was a hatchet-faced shrew who bargained ferociously in gold and goods, adding to her prosperity.

But I saw a small woman with bright intelligent eyes wearing a gown of madder-dyed linsey-woolsey. Her expression was tinged with a weary sadness, but she looked upon Farmer Wyatt with something else that I could not quite fathom. Was it humor?

George Wyatt smiled broadly. Who knew he had such sound teeth? "This lady hired our Abigail from me one day a week when she heard tell of my servant's talent with figuring. And now Mrs. Attley has allowed me to pay her court out on her farm. It is a goodly, blessed place! The biblical land of milk and honey, when compared with that windswept, barren heath amongst those warring families where I dwell, eh?

"And the lady deigned to accompany me this day, so that I might make proper peace with you. She compliments her holding, does she not? An angel of animal delivery, she is! Even runts survive. My heart is hers and she has made a better man of me.

"In short," he finally concluded, "I will cast that accursed butter churn into our bonfire tonight, gather up my animals, and join them to hers to begin a future together if she will have me. But she requires two things more. Those are, firstly for me to treat our Abigail as more daughter than servant and secondly, to make a true friend of you this St. John's Eve."

My answer waited for his hearing so long I'm sure he doubted my generosity. But it was the change in him that kept me mute. And the great torrent of his story needed time to digest, like a miracle.

The tears in his eyes hastened me along. "I forgive you with my whole heart," I assured my slanderer. "And I am delighted by your news and changed station in life and love, sir."

The lady of his affections touched my face gently. "I am Beatrice, Charlotte," she said quietly, as if she were still getting used to the sound of her own voice. "I knew your mother. She plucked my elder son from the sea once. Were it not for her, I would have lost him at twelve instead of twenty."

I curtseyed. "Thank you for the gift of knowing this, Madame."

"The least I could do is to help make things right between you and this man."

Our feasting together followed the reconciliation. Abigail rubbed her nose with William's in greeting. Then she leaned close to my ear and whispered, "Daughter or no, I'll reserve my right to accept attachment to another household--Captain Worthing's perhaps? I'll decide once the terms of my indenture are accomplished. Mayhap I will favor him only if the shy Captain Worthing agrees to make an offer for another widow of our mutual acquaintance, yes?"

"Why, Abigail. Have you set yourself up as matchmaker for the lonely of this island?"

"Nay! But I am poor, Mistress Charlotte. The poor are good observers, for we must seek opportunities for betterment. My master is not a bad man, only sometimes delivers himself to his fears and certain influences. I wish Widow Attley well with him, and I hope she is up to the task. As for me, I desired to be off that heath. He understood one thing, my poor blighted soul of a master. Evil dwells there."

Her master and his widow were calling her away on their continued walk down the Lower Path. I kept my voice quiet. "Of this I desire more knowledge."

"I value our association. I am at your service, Mistress Charlotte."

Chapter 18
The Bonfire

Randall's town crier bell called us all to the shoreline as the great St. John's Eve bonfire was lit. While low, the younger folk jumped over the flames. I did not join them. I remained earth-bound, watching the spectacle with my new brood of English children, feeling older than my years in the care of them.

My father stood guard over the flames, but smiled broadly as he looked back at me, with William raised high in my arms and Philip and Mary flanking my form. Mary's eyes shone with a look of disapproval, while Philip's gaze was one of pure longing, I thought. Why did the elders of their religion not allow children to play, I wondered.

The flames grew higher, and hands joined as the dancing around it began. Fear took over the look in Mary's eyes. But young Philip tapped his foot. My father grabbed my hand with his soot-stained one. "Come, children!" he called, pulling. "Around and around before we deliver that sleepyhead Will to his bed!"

And so, we joined the others around the fire.

The joy of our summer season was upon us. Our cousins soon fell into place in the circle.

"Are we dancing?" Mary asked nervously.

"Think of it as a procession," I tried.

"Not like any of ours going to Meeting! This is a merry one!" Philip observed, carefully copying the skipping steps of the other children.

Once we'd gone three times around, Bosun Riker began playing his tabor and Third Mate Archer his fiddle.

My father took William from my arms. "Stay, Charlotte. I'll get the rest to their slumbers. He nodded to a joyous figure among the dancers. "Randall will look after you and bring you home."

I danced hornpipes, fast and slow ones, with fellow young folks, and farmers and shipbuilders, planters, sailors and merchants, fisherfolk- migratory and permanent born in worlds both old and new. The arguments between the kings and queens of England and France, Spain and the Netherlands seemed very far away from here, where we would all soon be engaged in a summer of our common activity: bringing in the cod, salting it, loading the sack ships, and sending it off to other colonies. And if monarchs could settle their differences, we'd bring it to the countries of Europe, where even in wartime, people must eat.

The bonfire was beginning to die and form the ashes to nourish our summer gardens when Randall caught my hand. I loved the freedom I felt under his brotherly eyes. But those eyes were made more watchful by the secret we shared with my father and his fellow fishing admirals—that we were on the hunt for a murderer. I looked for Primus, for I was reminded of another secret that Randall and I held from Papa himself. I saw neither he nor his master. Mayhap Primus had gotten some free hours on this feast day to slip off to Manley's Cove. I hoped this to be true.

Home?" Randall asked.

"Home," I agreed, taking his offered hand.

I relished these moments alone with my friend as we began our trek, resting my head on Randall's shoulder as we walked.

"They say your sweet bread was the best put-out on St. John's Eve, little sister."

"That cannot be true."

"Perhaps your gift for hospitality lends to enjoyment? I wondered myself, for I have tasted your sweet breads past."

I swatted his arm just as a scream rose up from the shoreline.

We looked back. Both of us spotted a still form on the beach, wreathed in seaweed. He took my hand with urgency now, and we ran together towards the shore.

It was as if time itself had stopped. Where all was music and laughter, there was silence. A crowd had gathered around Abigail Barrie, Farmer George Wyatt's maid. She had been our guest that very afternoon. Abigail, so full of mirth and her own future plans. Randall and I fought our way through the circle of people surrounding her and knelt beside the girl who had become our friend. She seemed a creature of the sea, her soul already going to their depths, her lips tinged blue.

But there. A bubble of air.

"Help me turn her," I commanded Randall. He did, despite mutterings of "T'aint decent" and "leave the poor lass be."

But I sensed strongly that the "poor lass" did not wish to be. She wished to breathe. "There. On her side, so," I further instructed Randall, who did not question, but did as I bid him. Another bubble from those lips gone the color of marsh violets.

I took a hold of those capable shoulders and thumped her back.

Nothing.

"Hold fast," Randall had me brace her now. He took my place and whacked her harder.

An explosion of seawater erupted from our mermaid's mouth, along with a hearty "Oww!"

She sat up, blinked twice, and touched her back. "I'll be sore for a week!" she sputte.

Randall and I were both weeping, else we would have chastised her for ingratitude. Abigail looked around at the crowd beyond us, half of them murmuring in wonder, the rest speaking of dark forces afoot. Through them pushed Captain Worthing.

"I fear I have lost the dory you lent me, sir," Abigail told him. "With its steady ballasted bottom."

"No matter, child. No matter at all," he said, through tears of his own.

He wrapped his fine wool coat around her as she told her tale to our hushed merrymakers. "I had a desire to see the bonfire from the water, you see. What a sight it was, with the dancing shadows in a great circle around it! I wished to join them, but I had to tell Charlotte Jaddore something. What was it? Something important. I might catch her at home, where I saw her walking with her father and the children. I thought, if I rowed hard enough, I might have her attention before she was abed. But you are here, Charlotte. How did you get here so fast from your home?"

"It was not I, but my cousin with my father and the children, Abigail," I sought to untangle her confused mind. "Mary English and I are almost the same in height."

"Oh, aye, aye." She laughed. "I am not fully drowned daft then?"

"No, indeed. You seem as sensible as ever."

She looked out over the dying St. John's Eve fire. "Where is my sea monster?"

"Monster?"

"He lifted me above the waves."

"A dolphin, mayhap?" I'd heard of such things from my father's sailors.

"Mayhap. But what was it sent me into the water? How did I come to be cast overboard? There was no swell. The sea was like glass. But for a shadow."

"Shadow?" Captain Worthing asked.

"Aye. Behind me, sir. Of a great antlered stag. But that could not be, could it?"

Awed whispers rose up around us. "The stag. The Mummer Stag," they claimed. "The Christmas Mummer Stag, come back to bring more misfortune upon us!"

Randall grunted. "Your stag did not come from out of the sea," he said. "It came from within the boat."

"Aye," Third Mate Archer agreed, as he lifted a dripping oilskin that had followed her ashore. "Under this. What you thought ballast was your attacker, lass."

"Was it?" Abigail reached up behind her right ear. Her fingers came away bloody. Her eyes went up into her head then, and her frame shook with a terrible violence, before she fell against Captain Worthing's steady chest.

Captain Worthing staunched the bleeding with his handkerchief, then carried Abigail to our home, into the small, windowless room behind our kitchen hearth. I found my vial of hartshorn to place under her nose. She came to herself again, to the relief of us all. I sent Randall upstairs to my clothes press, so that I could replace Abby's soaked gown with some of my nightclothes. I then sent the men into the front of the house.

The borning room, my mother called the small, spare chamber where I now made our new guest comfortable. It had a treasured place in her heart. Whereas I was tossed into this world on a wave, my hale and beautiful brother first saw light in its warm and peaceful confines. And tonight I had learned of another lad, Beatrice Attley's son, who my mother once pulled from the sea. I had another story of the brave woman who loved my father. It served to keep me calm as I asked my brother's joy-filled spirit to look after my friend.

As if answering my prayer Captain Worthing stood in the doorway.

"You have done us all a great service, Charlottle Jaddore," he said softly. "And have a protector in me, if any should say otherwise."

"You have admired our young friend since my trial, I think, Captain."

"She puts me in mind of a bright-minded daughter I lost to a wave of yellow fever that also struck down her mother."

"Oh, sir. May Our Lord hold them close to his heart." It was sometimes hard for me to remember that my father's fellow merchants did not blithely sail the seas, without the loss and sorrows that inflict the lives of the rest of us. No wonder the tears in his eyes, if he thought our clever matchmaker lost to us.

Captain Worthing took the light coverlet from my hands. "Randall gathers information from those still on the beach," he informed me. "Take your own rest, Charlotte," he urged. "The night watch is mine. I will call you if you are needed."

I had one more task in the front room before turning to the stairs. I spread out Abigail's sea-soaked clothes beside its hearth fire, turning over our eventful St. John's Eve in my mind. I would give a detailed account to my father in the morning.

I had just put out Abigail's stockings on the stones when I heard two men's voices outside the window. I stopped, listened.

"The Mummer Stag has come again."

"Nay. No spirit knocked the sense from Abigail Barrie. Better to ask who among us might be dark enough to escape her notice and hide as ballast in a boat?"

"An Indian? One of the black sailors? Or Primus, maybe?"

"The oilskin cover was over her attacker. He did not have to be a black or Portuguese or Mi'kmaq. This is how rumors hatch, man. Calm yourself!"

"With such evil dwelling in our midst? First the fire, then a cliffside fall, now something heaving children into the sea? I must look after my own!"

"What was the maid set to tell Charlotte Jaddore, do you think?"

"Aye! What has that Witch of Avalon to do with this?"

"Hush now!" The voice lowered. "Do not you call her that in her father's presence!"

"What else do you call that many-tongued wench, her potions, her Indian magic?"

"Some are calling her saint, who brings the drowned back to life."

"Humph. Abigail Barrie has the strength of three of our womenfolk. She alone coughed out that seawater and got a sore back for her trouble from those two strange ones."

"Oh? Randall Kelly is a witch now too?"

"What if he paints spells with his likenesses of birds and bluffs and folk? He's Irish and a papist."

"'Tis not the pope sent the lass into the depths."

"But someone did."

"We needs put the home squabbles away here, says our fishing admiral."

"Aye, we've got thieving heathen Indians to contend with. And witch's spawn from that nest of evil in Salem."

"Let's hope Abigail Barrie has a head hard enough to survive a bash and drowning both. Strong enough to figure a name for the one who sent her into the sea."

"She had a name—the Mummer Stag!"

"A specter? Or a man?"

"If a man, he's never come forth. The other mummers of Christmas—the hobby horse and dancing clowns, they were all guessed out by our neighbors. But none knew the tall fellow who cavorted with them. And he never showed himself, remember?"

"He may have been a stilt walker."

"Or a spirit of the air, I tell you, conjured up by dark forces."

The footsteps moved on down the lane. To whom did they belong? I could not identify them. Randall could have. I wished him beside me. Were those two the only ones saying such things? How many more might be having similar, but unspoken thoughts?

Even as I felt tears forming in the corners of my eyes, I was glad that my father and cousins were tucked away in their beds as the talk of ghosts and witches infected the early hours of St. John's Day.

The next day began with Captain Dunbar banging at our door, demanding that the Fishing Admirals call a meeting.

"Calm yourself," my father, fresh from learning of our additional house members, demanded.

"When two of the three of the admirals are here, conspiring against me? Against me and my beloved countess both?"

Captain Worthing placed a hand on the aggrieved man's shoulder and bade him sit by the hearth. "There is no such conspiracy, sir. Kindly keep your voice moderate. We are caring for an injured child."

"Child? She is a servant who does not know her place! For all I know she feigned all her mishap and injury to draw attention away! That is precisely the matter!" He seemed to realize suddenly, targeting me under his gaze. She may be in league with your daughter and that crippled crier of yours, Martin Jaddore!"

"What are you talking about? In league to do what, man?"

"To steal my Primus away from me! He has disappeared!"

My father and his fishing admirals did as they were bid. They met to discuss the missing Primus. Missing, for they refused to call him out as ran away of his own accord to seek his freedom. A searching party was formed, led by Gideon and Sam Brewster in the spirit of neighborliness. But Captain Dunbar's other neighbor, George Wyatt, failed to rouse himself for their hard horse rides and inquiries along the shore. They dared not go many miles inland for fear of disturbing relations with the Beothuk. Instead, my father sent word of the search for the wanted man through their Mi'kmaq ambassador, Darting Badger.

"A good choice, do you think?" he asked Randall and I pointedly.

"Oh, aye sir. No better man than our Darting Badger!" Randall proclaimed with enough false enthusiasm to throw my father's look sideways.

He circled us as he sometimes did to errant members of his crew. "Not a trace of the man, even around fishing spots he'd been known to frequent in years gone by, like Manley's Cove."

"Is that so, sir?"

"It is. Of course, some three ships left the harbor before Primus was discovered missing this morning. Ships bound for distant ports, both foreign and within the colonies. If such a man as Primus proves himself useful, I can't imagine any of them willing to give him up. So that is a possibility, do you agree?"

"Oh, aye, sir."

"Hmm. And my dear daughter, you have said nothing at all. Do you not wish to join in our conjecture?"

"We are sorry our friend is being slandered, sir," I took up my father's challenge, even though Randall's look told me to keep silent.

"Slandered? How so?"

"He is being called out as the Christmas Mummer, suspected of the assault on our Abigail."

"Aye, his timing was not good on that account. But I think we all saw things that his master did not. We all saw a man bursting for his freedom. By land or sea."

"How long do you suppose the search will continue sir?" Randall ventured.

"With the French settlement at Plaisance so near? With the English harassing them while they tell us to keep to our fishing? With the native people still recovering from the case against two of their own? I do not think the search will be successful on land or sea."

He caught the small smiles that crept over both our faces then, for my father was a clever man.

Chapter 19
Abigail's Stay

My father had our house built when he and my mother were full of hope for a family. Rooms that filled with merchant goods instead of children on either side of his quarters made way for people as we gave shelter to our English cousins and now added a recovering Abigail Barrie.

My child-caring responsibilities grew lighter as our invalid guest delved into a treasure of amusements to keep little William close by her even while she was abed in the borning room.

Little Will delighted in her finger puzzles and string games, her songs, and stories. Once she felt strong enough to be about, with infinite patience she guided him in simple tasks like sweeping the hearth and rolling bits of pastry.

His sister Mary, of course, disapproved. "These are not tasks for boy children," she admonished from her sewing corner by the window, where she was overseeing Philip's study of The Common Rudiments of Latin Grammar.

Abigail only laughed. "Those who can cook will never starve. And should not everyone know where the broom is?"

As if to punctuate her contentions, my father put his head in the kitchen doorway. "Ship-shape, crew?" he asked. "Ready for assessment, are we?"

"Aye, Cap!" little Will said, saluting smartly, bringing a smile to even his sister's face.

My father put his hands behind his back as he inspected the flour-dusted kitchen. William climbed off my lap to do the same, Papa's small shadow.

"How do you fare this day, Mistress Barrie?" the captain of our vessel asked our bread baker.

"Too well to take any more advantage of your hospitality, sir. I should be returning to my duties up on the cliff."

"It grieves me to hear it, for I deem you a light-bearer, like my own Charlotte." He peered around the small bandage left above her ear. "Some healing needed yet, I think."

"And I believe you see it with your heart's eye, dear sir."

"Is there any other way to see?" he challenged her. "*Mais non!*" He tapped his finger to his lips. "I insist you are not to leave us without first consulting the grandmothers."

"The grandmothers, Captain?"

"Yes, Demas and Nakuset, Charlotte's medicine teachers. They have broad and deep knowledge of restoring health. Besides, Charlotte needs to replenish her supplies of my favorite mushrooms. The visit will require a trip inland. I will talk with Darting Badger about arrangements for the journey- when you are stronger."

"But my master—"

"You will leave the matter of George Wyatt to me, if it pleases you. I have informed him to transfer both good cow Colley and your much-improved butter churn here to our own acreage. You may take up limited milkmaid duties, supervised, of course, to make sure those duties are not over-taxing. Your master will find his own path until you are ready to resume your place in his employ."

Abigail lowered her head in surrender. "If it pleases you, sir."

He turned on his heal. Behind him, Little Will did the same.

"It pleases me very much," he answered.

"Very much!" his shadow affirmed.

"Come, Will, young Philip," my father called out to the boys. "Inspection of the animals, next!"

My father took great joy in commanding the brood under his roof. The restlessness I'd often seen demonstrated while he was on shore was not apparent that summer. And his lording over the household duties was a welcome relief from his responsibilities surrounding the evidence of violence in our midst. Whatever their circumstances, ages, or various stations in life, Papa's generous heart expanded to accommodate our home's numbers. He was now captain of a land crew. And he loved and cared for us as he did the crew of the *Esperance.*

After we enjoyed our midday meal together the following day, Papa announced more news for our Abigail. "It is my understanding that your master has brought your household and the other animals off your cliffside. He dwells in the lowland around Conception Bay at present."

She grinned wide now. "Does he, sir?"

"And worry not. He is not starving in your absence."

"The esteemed lady has made good then?"

"To wed? Possible, or so says St. John's crier. This is a detail our Randall has not yet managed to confirm. But, to lodge with the widow who has captured his heart? It has been accomplished."

"Then he is the most fortunate of men, sir."

"The most changed of men, it seems to me, thanks to the influence of the two women in his life."

"Influence?"

"Aye, lass."

My father's laughter stopped abruptly. I did not like the nature of the silence that followed. I looked up from Abigail's cutting out pieces of Partridgeberry tart to see my father reach for her arm. "What's wrong? Are you ailing?"

"A nudging inside my head is all, sir. It's like something that I left in the water, that struggles to come to the surface of my mind. If I may sit."

"Here, here, then," he led her to his oak wainscot chair with its boxed seat and tufted cushion's comfort. Charlotte!" he called me over.

I sat with our guest and felt around the small bandage. "Tender still?" I asked.

"A little."

"Does your head ache you?"

"Sometimes. In the night. When things are quiet." She gave me a rueful smile. "And when I am thinking too hard."

Of her time in the water, I could see it in her eyes.

"Your meals continue to agree with you?"

"Oh, aye. I take great enjoyment in the victuals here. After the heavings of the first few days you all so kindly tended me, I rarely take sick now."

"We wish to help return you to that good health," my father said, worry still lacing his voice. "Will, my lad- bring the footstool for Mistress Barrie!"

"Red?" he asked.

"Just so, the red one, crewman!"

"Aye, aye, Cap!" William saluted, before pushing the red quilted stool that was half his small size, until it was under Abigail's feet.

"If this household is any better to me I shall stay the season, Captain," she teased.

"Nothing would give us greater pleasure."

She laughed outright then. "But I must be of use. My primary talent is not needed here. Your account books do not require much second scrutiny, sir, as Charlotte already does an admirable job."

"But we are all engaged with the high season's fishing work. And we needs must calculate the colonies which need our cod most, now that the French ports are banned to us"

"Marylanders are Catholic, sir, and observe meat fasting days," she offered.

"There, just so! Do you not see how valuable to us you are?"

I knew that Maryland has many miles of its own Atlantic shoreline and inland waterways, but I did not seek to dampen my dear father's enthusiasm as he continued. "Besides, our harvesting will begin soon. Having you among us at the store and keeping track of the credit lines of the people with whom we do business is of great value to us all."

"'Tis the truth my esteemed sire speaks," I insisted. "And this tart contains the last of our dried partridgeberry supply, Abigail. Soon we can build up your strength as we roam the hills for this summer's berries before the birds will have them."

"And my mushrooms. Do not you forget my mushrooms," Papa insisted.

"Well, if my master does not object—"

"Object?" George Wyatt poked his head through the top of our double Dutch door, holding out a bouquet of wildflowers. "Why, how might I object when your travail has brought me closer to winning the heart of my beloved?"

I was still getting used to Farmer Wyatt's new mellow personhood. The gift of flowers went so beyond his transformation, I had to sit myself down with them festooned in my lap while Mary brought a jar to contain them.

Then his betrothed also appeared, looking fresh as a summer day after the rain in her indigo striped gown with intricate embroidery trim on its linen jacket.

The Widow Atley soon had my arm on a walk around my medicinal garden. But Constance Atley was not there to speak of herbs, teas, and tinctures. "You'd think with all the males on this island, I would have a better choice. Mayhap I waited too long. George Wyatt has a touch of the fool about him, but he is not a bad man, Charlotte. And do not you laugh, but I like the tone of his voice and the way he puts words together. My. Is that enough? That he fills the silences I had grown used to with his beautiful voice and sentiments? Well, no matter. We are neither of us growing younger and the bible says that man was not meant to be alone. That is why I insisted he make proper amends and get back in your good graces. Still, I cannot yet wed him."

"Why is that Mrs. Atley?"

"Because there is something he holds back."

"What might that be?"

"The source of his fear."

"Fear?" I thought of the talk of the Witch of Avalon. "Of me?"

"I think not. Fear of whoever put accusing you into his mind."

"You think his allegation was not his idea alone?"

"He says it was. But I have my doubts. And he will get no further in his suit until I learn the truth of it. That means a full confession. But I wanted you to know you have no more worries from him since I allowed him a place away from those cliffs."

I turned my gaze up from my medicine garden to the cliffs in question. "It is a place of sadness."

"More than sadness. Danger. Of a fall in the fog. Or worse. People are talking, Charlotte. That more than an accident might have brought James Brewster off that cliff. That the same purveyor of evil sought to harm our Abigail. Talk of dark forces, too, that the fishing admirals are seeking to uncover."

As we walked, I thought of Rose and her heavy courting-gift boots. Of Master Brewster working on his new will and testament as the ink blotted around his fingers. His sons' treachery against the Beothuk. And Captain Dunbar and his Bermuda cedar, saving sailors and fishermen from British impressment during wartime, but using them to build ships that will transport people from African nations into lives of slavery. My father and his truth-seeking admirals seemed outmatched by all of it.

Chapter 20
Summer's End

"Charlotte, what are you doing?" Mary demanded.

"Harvesting our first corn."

"Harvesting? But the stalks have not yet reached even to our middles."

I exchanged a smile with Abigail, standing in the field with our baskets. "Ours is Gaspe corn," I explained to my cousin. "Its planting and harvest were taught to us by my Mi'kmaq relatives."

"It is a variety that suits our climate and soil," Abby explained further. "Gaspe has a faster growing season—these ears may be short and stubby, but they are ready and sweet in half the time most corn needs to ripen."

Mary plucked an ear off its stalk and examined it closely. She felt along the outside of the stalk.

"Does it feel full?" I asked her.

She nodded. "Aye."

"And look," Abigail directed," the silks have died back and are dry, see?"

"Good signs. But the revealing will tell." She peeled back the last layer to reveal a full cob of golden hued kernels.

"And now, the only proof remaining," Abigail proclaimed before she bit into the cob, chewed, swallowed. "Perfect! Oh Charlotte, what a gift was bestowed on us all by your mother's people!"

I was touched by the way she expressed her enthusiastic thanks. Perhaps our friend had known hunger in her young life.

"We should leave some on the cob to dry and make popped corn for little William," I suggested.

Mary frowned. "Popped corn," she said. "As insubstantial as laughter."

Abigil's beautiful, musical mirth came to my rescue once more. "Aye, Mary! And just as important for easing us through this veil of tears!"

I cleared my way to another stalk, bent it down, and snapped it off. "And look, the beans are climbing the strong stalks, and the squash has kept the weeds away below all."

"I love a summer's bounty," Abby said, "and treasure it more that it is so much a shorter season than the ones of home, which I must admit are now fading from my memories," There was a hint of wistfulness in her voice. "We can add fresh berries to our porridge too, can we not, Charlotte? May we gather some? I feel strong enough to climb the hills with you and the children."

I marveled at our guest's resilience, but also felt protective of her. What to give her as an answer? That balance is what all parents must feel daily. I was in awe of it, and fearful of making a mistake in judgement. But when I saw my young friend's radiant smile, I had an inkling of the joys of raising a family, too.

"I will consult with Papa," I dodged my way around her request for the time being.

As busy as all were around the cod fishing, salting and harvest, the return of the whales off our peninsula's shores was always met with excursions to our cliffs to view their antics. That year it came in mid-July. Our expanded family was joined by Captain Worthing, who was a frequent visitor, looking after the recovering Abigail and consulting with her in his now active courtship of the Widow Gavin.

"I was in hopes that the lady might join us," he said to their go-between.

Abby smiled. "I conveyed the invitation, sir, to both Mrs. Gavin and Mrs. Brewster. But Rose was taken poorly this morning, so Mrs. Gavin decided to stay behind to tend to her."

"Admirable," Captain Worthing replied, without hiding the disappointment in his voice.

"She asked me to deliver this, sir," Abigail said, handing over a small note. Reading it was the source of Captain

Worthing's improvement in disposition, I believe.

But I was left with wondering if the real reason the two didn't join our outing was because two fishing admirals and I, all of us trying to come to conclusions about Master Brewster's death, would have his wife and housekeeper under scrutiny. I did not like the fact that such thoughts invaded my mind.

We took a small meal with us for a day watching the humpbacks breaching. The ocean churned to whitewater by the feet and wings of the murre and our beloved sea parrots, while the sky filled with auks and black-legged kittiwakes.

"Do you ever think of joining those who hunt the whales?" Captain Worthing asked my father.

"No. Not after I have seen them like this, at play with their young. I understand the Inuit natives to our north, their need of the hunt. But the whale is a sacred animal to them, providing all. Our fishers use little more than the blubber and the baleen."

"Aye. The rest is discarded."

"And we are seeing fewer of these magnificent creatures by the year, are we not?"

"You have...interesting thoughts, Martin," Captain Worthing said, with a hint of unease in his voice.

Papa laughed. "You are not the first to make that observation, sir."

My father's favorites were the golden-headed gannets. He took out his spyglass to watch their dances in wonder. I saw traces of what he looked like when he courted my mother, I think, when he told us of how her eyes shone whenever she scanned the horizon.

"I knew I had a brave adventurer in my arms then," he said, "with no fear of the watery or land worlds around. Now, how was I to convince her to do it all with me?"

"The *Esperance*!" Philip guessed.

"*Exactement,* my lad! So I set sail with my brave maid of the waves."

"I shall do the same, cousin," Philip predicted. "I shall plow the waves, not the ground!"

"And find your mate on the journey?"

He made a sour face. "Oh, if I must."

My father laughed. "You must if your hearts match. If you share this dream."

It was late summer before our Abby was deemed hearty enough to venture with my English cousins into the forest. Our berry, mushroom, and wildflower gatherings would also be a chance for us to listen to the woodland birds. Our guide inland was Darting Badger, who had become a frequent enough trading visitor to our house that even Philip seemed at ease in his presence. The unfortunate circumstances of their first meeting forgotten, they were becoming fast friends.

As the trees closed in around us, the mushrooms my father craved appeared everywhere—among the leaves, hiding among the barks of downed trees, sprouting out in the loamy soil. I took out my linen sack and showed the children how to adjust their eyes and see the hidden bounty of the forest around.

Delighted, they set off in all directions on their hunt.

But I did not let them put any of their finds in my sack until I had inspected them, in the ways my grandmother had taught me.

When Philip selected one that looked like a meadow mushroom, Darting Bader grasped his wrist and brought him to my side. I nodded my thanks to our observant guide and called the children together. Then I turned over the stem to reveal the gills. I put one of my own finds beside it. The gills must be pink, or you have chosen a dangerous imposter," I told them. "And see how the flesh stains?" I pressed it against my sack to reveal a yellow blotch. "Yellow, orange, or red, and it is a poisonous cousin to our rings of meadow mushroom."

"We do not want it then?"

"No. I keep only mushrooms that do no harm when eaten raw or cooked. We must thank Darting Badger for his keen eyes."

Without further prompting, Philip bowed to our woodland guide. "Thank you, sir," he said.

I smiled. "Look at little William's funny puffballs. I used to confuse them with other dangerous mushrooms, who, in their young button stage, are like puffballs, until my grandmothers showed me to cut them in half." I did so. "See? William's puffball is all white. The dangerous impostors show faint color. Look carefully."

I placed my face close to William's. "All white?"

"All white, Car-lot!" he reported.

"It may enter my sack, then, for my papa's soup. Ah, look, under those trees, a lovely stand of blue chanterelle!" I nodded toward the incurved edged cluster of ridged, blue-back fused together clusters.

"Oh, I do hope we can eat those, Mistress Charlotte," Abby cried. They are so pretty!"

"After cooking, their taste is most pleasant," I was happy to report.

As we got deeper into the woods, our guide asked us to sit beneath an ancient balsam and wait quietly. Within minutes he parted the graceful low hung branches. Walking on each other's arms were my beloved grandmothers, smiling ear to ear. Darting Badger had conveyed my request for them to look at Abigail's injury, but I was not sure until that moment that they would agree to meet us.

They were a study in opposites. Demas, my Beothuk great grandmother, was tall in the way of her people and carried her height proudly, like the great sturdy trees around us. Her hair was as white as the clouds of summer. She walked by the side of my Mi'kmaq grandmother, Nakuset, who barely reached her shoulder. Nakuset's shining black hair had only streaks of silver. Like most of the Mi'kmaq, she was more used to the company of the people from across the Atlantic, so she cast her air of calmness over her elder, who was shy among strangers. "These children are our relatives," she assured Demas, "because they belong to the people of Wavewalker."

I took Abby's hand and sat her before my grandmothers "And this is our friend, Abigail, who has had an injury this past St. John's Eve, while on the sea."

"Have her sit," Nakuset told me.

Abigail kept her hold on my hand after she did so.

"They will do you no harm," I promised, as my grandmothers lit a smudge stick of wrapped bunchberry and began to pass it over her body. She let go of me. Nodding to assure our friend, I left her to my grandmothers and their wisdom.

Nakuset and Demas both circled Abigail with the dried bunchberry smoke before they lifted her hair to see to her injured spot. Then they pressed the smoking remains into a whelk shell, stepped back and consulted with each other in a mix of Beothuk and Mi'kmaq languages that I found difficult to follow.

Nakuset grinned before she said, in English. "Ho! A head full of numbers, this one!"

Abigail looked astonished. "How do you know that, Ma'am?"

"The way you count the beads on our capes. When troubled, we take comfort in things we love. You love to count, *oui*?"

"I do, aye, Ma'am."

The women nodded to each other before Nakuset spoke for them again. "And your fear of us, it is not so great now?"

"No." Abby smiled. "Not so great."

"Good!" Her ear ornaments tinkled. "You can hear us, then. My elder and I wish you to know some things. Your eyes are clear of the injury bestowed on you."

"Bestowed?"

"Yes. You know someone did this to you?"

"Well, I—"

"You were felled, young one. By someone not thinking in the right way."

"I see."

"Good."

It occurred to me then that we should have consulted with my grandmothers on James Brewster's fall from the cliff.

Grandmother Nakuset spoke again. "What remains is..." she paused here, a pause that Demas filled in with a brief torrent of words in the Beothuk language. "Your heart sickness, Demas says."

"Heart sickness?"

Demas spoke softly now in her own language. She gestured with her hands before Abigail's face.

"Yes, that's it!" Abby agreed. "'Tis akin to a veil, a dark veil before my eyes, and I cannot see behind it! Sometimes I shake with my effort to remember."

Demas nodded. Then the grandmothers consulted again before Nakuset spoke. "You drink a tea made with yellow rattle?"

"Oh, aye. Charlotte brews it up for me every afternoon."

"Good: Nakuset looked my way. "Do you need more?" she asked.

"I have plenty, Grandmother,"

"All is well. Be content, Wavewalker. This one, she is a good healer."

"Yes," I agreed. Only then did I realize I had been holding my breath.

"Good, then. Let's find some fruit. Winter is coming, children."

My grandmothers gave us each a basket for our berrying. Little William's was a perfect fit for his small hands. He patted Grandmother Demas's soft Caribou skin apron in thanks, making her laugh. She led us on a winding path to higher ground and a grove of wild blueberry bushes gleaming with fruit.

At the top of the hill we rested. Soon, good ears and patience combined for a reward of visitors, the birds. We heard warblers of many varieties of color and song. They were all around us. The curious finch was near tame. At my grandmothers' signal, I did as they had schooled me back when I was the youngest one in their company— with soft murmurings I coaxed one to a small mound of black huckleberries in William's outstretched hand. We all held our breath.

My smallest cousin stayed so remarkably still! A thought occurred to me that I said aloud, once the bird finally left his finger with her prize.

"Why William, I would not have believed you could have had the patience to draw a bird when first you came to us. You are a two-year wonder."

"He is no longer two," came the voice of his sister.

William turned and held up two berry-stained little fingers, confused. "I not two, May-ree?" he asked her.

"No, you have achieved three years, little William."

"Indeed?" I proclaimed. "When did he turn three?" I asked Mary.

"Thursday last." She anticipated my next question with a firm look. "We do not celebrate birthdays, cousin. We celebrated his birth. That will do."

Philip patted Will's cheek. "I remember your birthday, little brother," he said. "Father brought in some fireweed and aster flowers from the field to celebrate our new William. And Mother made you a fine lace cap."

Grandmother Nakuset translated our talk to her fellow grandmother. Demas began tapping out a heartbeat rhythm on her apron and the two began a song of celebration. We clapped along, even Mary. I placed a sprig of woodland angelica behind our new three-year-old's ear.

"I three, Cousin Car-lot!" William proclaimed, holding his little basket aloft.

"Indeed you are, my fine fellow," I proclaimed.

Abby laughed. "I shall take up your baby blouse and make you a set of trousers, little one," she decided.

My grandmothers had provided his third birthday celebration, and even gifts of baskets and berries for us all. The wonder of it made my heart soar.

"And now you can call the birds to you," Nakuset told him. "That is a great power."

Each of my grandmothers took our new three years child by the shoulders then and pressed their foreheads to his. My Beothuk grandmother made a quiet pronouncement which my Mi'kmaq grandmother translated. "My spirit sister says he is Skyheart now. This is a good day!"

Darting Badger returned to accompany my grandmothers home. The three slipped back into the forest as silently as they had entered out presence. We began our mushroom and berry-laden return journey.

"Do they live in those trees, Cousin Charlotte?" Philip asked.

I smiled. "Among the trees, yes, in houses covered with the bark of the birch. And in winter Grandmother Demas and I live in a cozy lodge underground."

"I should like to visit you in winter."

"And you would be--

"What did she mean, power?" Mary interrupted our conversation. "And what is this name, Skyheart?"

"It is an honor, bestowed on little William because of his connection to the bird that came to him. Our traditions gift us with many names and variations."

"Did she mean that William has power from that finch?"

"The Mi'kmaq and Beothuk believe we are kin to the animals, Mary," I said carefully, praying for guidance in my words. "That we are like them, that they are like us. Learning their language helps us to be able to be close to them. the sky people."

"Sky people?"

"Yes. They think of birds the way we think of ... well, angels, mayhap."

A squirrel darted onto our path. Abigail and the boys tracked it, following. Mary took the opportunity to move closer to me. She lowered her voice. "We are taught that to do such things—to bring the birds so close-- is witchcraft."

I breathed deeply before I spoke. "You have seen it done. What do you think now?"

"I—I think I saw observation. Intense observation. And stillness. That is how calling a bird to a person's finger is achieved."

"And it can be done by a three-year-old child."

"A child under the influence of witches, Reverend Mather might say."

I took another deep breath. "Mary. Do you believe my grandmothers to be witches?"

"No. But my home is so different than this place. Oh, why did that bird have to be yellow?"

"I do not understand."

She wrung her hands now as she walked. "There are marks on your body. They frighten me."

We shared a sleeping chamber. She had seen them, of course. "My smallpox scars?"

"Is that what they are?"

"Yes, Mary. It is the sickness that killed my mother and brother. Has the pox never visited Salem?"

"It has. But I did not think. My mind made them something else. Witches' teats. Witches give suck to their familiars. Cats, Dogs. Birds. Yellow birds."

"Mary."

"I ask your forgiveness, cousin."

"Oh, Mary," I said her name again, unable, in that moment, to grant what she sought of me.

Chapter 21
Escape to New York

We expected my father to celebrate our return from our journey inland, but I knew that troubled look he wore while rising from his seat at his mahogany desk. Still, he laughed when little William jumped into his arms.

"I three, Captain Papa!" he exulted.

Mary set him down on his sturdy little legs. "Yes, you are a full three years, brother. That is old enough to know that this man is your cousin, not your papa," she told him sternly.

William's little chin quivered at her chastisement. "Captain?" he asked of me now.

"Yes, darling boy. My papa is still our captain," I assured him.

"Our own father and mother are in Boston," his sister continued her lesson with her youngest brother. "Where are they?" she commanded his repetition.

He pondered.

"New York," my father answered for him.

"York!" William said brightly.

Mary directed William to the little stool we kept for him in my father's study room and handed him a spool of wool. Then she rushed to my father's side, Her eyes were searching the top of his desk. "You have heard from our parents?"

"Of them, Mary."

Philip joined his sister. "Why are they in New York, Cousin Martin? Did they send us more packages? Letters?" he wanted to know.

"Not this time."

In the silence, Mary rested her hand behind Philip's neck. "You said that you heard 'of them.' Oh, cousin, are they—?"

"No, no!" my father assured her. "They live. Your parents have fled. Escaped from their jailers, as they were summoned to trial in Salem. They are in New York, on the island of Manhattan."

Mary sat. "May God protect them. They have forfeited their bond fee. They are fugitives now."

"I fear so. They have not risked sending you packages, or even a letter. But they send their love to you by way of the quartermaster of the *Hollyhock*, who is a gentleman of our mutual acquaintance. They are safe, abiding with friends in New York. Influential friends. And they are in a royal colony that we are confident will not give them up no matter the commands from Massachusetts Bay. That is all we know. I am sorry that the news is not better or carries more detail."

Philip reached for my father, touching his slashed sleeve. "Let us go there! We can find them in New York City, Captain. Let us bring them and our Susanna here, with us."

"They still hope the madness will pass, Philip. It appears they are willing to wait for justice to be served. They remain determined to return to your home to Salem, despite..."

"Despite what, Papa?" I asked.

"The worsening of persecution, the spreading of accusations." He turned to our eldest cousin now. "Mary, supper is waiting for us on the kitchen hearth, by way of a gracious gift of it from the Widow Gavin. Will you and Philip go upstairs and consult our bible, dear heart? Might you find a good prayer for us to offer together tonight upon the occasion of our hopes for your parents' and sister's deliverance?"

"Yes, sir," she answered, leading her brother toward the stairs.

My father's step was heavy beside mine as he carried little Will into the kitchen and set him on one of his favorite tasks—pouring water. This time it was to wash traces of mud and leaves over our bounty of fruit. My father had not even asked about the mushroom harvest waiting in the bag beside the hearth. We stood on either side of William, gathering strength, I think, from his child's wonder of the task at hand. As he finished, my father wiped his chubby wet fingers with a cloth.

"So, you have had a birthday, have you, darling boy?"

"Aye, Cap! I three!"

"We must take the measure of you, must we not, Charlotte?"

I was so lost in my thoughts of what was happening to our south and to the English family, that I barely realized he was handing me a piece of charred wood from the fireplace and pressing Will's back against the stairwell wall. My yearly growth rate was recorded there, as were three marks of my brother's growing.

Little Will took his place, still and stouthearted, and watched, wide-eyed as my father recorded his name beside the mark. He then ran off to proclaim his honor to his siblings.

I busied myself stirring the fragrant asparagus flavored stew that the Widow Gavin had left us in our hearth's cauldron.

"Have there been more hangings, Papa?" I finally asked.

My father sighed hard but did not attempt to shield me from the news he'd kept from the English children. "Yes. Many more hangings. And even a pressing."

"Pressing?"

"I had to ask the quartermaster about it myself, it is so rarely used now. It is called *peine forte et dure*. If a defendant stands mute before his accusers, thus refusing to be judged by them, he is forced to withstand heavier and heavier stones placed upon his chest. A Salem farmer refused to enter a plea, thus keeping the magistrates from confiscating his land."

"What happened?"

"He endured days of this torture, and died, leaving his land to his sons."

"Oh, Papa," I breathed out my horror.

I left the stew bubbling and reached into my canvas bag, selecting the mushrooms with the mildest flavor to tie up and dry above the hearth. My father was still so lost in his thoughts of what was happening in Salem, that he merely began cutting lengths of string for me without comment.

"In another case, a husband and wife were both judged guilty, and the husband, despite his petitions to Boston authorities, was hanged. The wife's hanging was postponed, only because the babe had quickened in her womb. A child who will be born an orphan before they take even his mother from him."

"How terrible."

"Indeed. Perhaps these two cases convinced Philip and Mary to leave for New York. The plea for their escape came straight from their church's Boston pulpit itself. So, all is not lost. They have friends. And their lives. But young Mary is correct, they have lost their bond, and their Salem house and goods were confiscated. Ransacked, even."

I glanced down upon him from my place at the drying rack. "Oh, Papa. Those children."

"Our children now and perhaps forever. We must not give them up, Charlotte."

"Of course not."

Papa breathed in the steaming, fulsome flavor of our soup. "Add some of your meadow mushrooms?" he suggested. So. He had noticed our mushroom gatherings.

I smiled. "Of course." And did so.

"A fine harvest. I am deeply grateful for your efforts, *mon onge*, and for the wisdom Demas and Nakuset have imparted. Did they appear out of the forest?"

"They did indeed, with gifts, and a great fondness for all, especially our Will."

"Ah, who could not? His joy in every moment is so wondrous that it... well, it pains my heart sometimes."

I left my task and took his hand. "I feel that as well, dear Papa. And I miss him too."

He squeezed my hand. "The boys seem to be adjusting well to our clime and our ways. But I worry about Mary."

"Yes, I do too," I agreed, silently resolving to forgive my cousin her slights and suspicions. I prayed to widen my heart, for she might soon become my sister.

Chapter 22
Abigail Remembers

The next morning Abby awoke in good health but, it seemed to me, with a troubled mind. She waited until my father led the English children to a cove on an excursion to view a beached whale, one whose presence Randall had announced to us before he cried it out to all of St. John's. As we cleared the table of our breakfast bowls, Abby took my hand.

"It is a quiet time in the house, Charlotte. Might we talk?"

"Of course."

We took seats on either side of the kitchen fire. "After our wonderful day yesterday, I woke up remembering," she said quietly. "Remembering what I had need to tell you that night of St. John's Eve."

"Ah. Did my grandmothers' confidence in your healing help?"

"It must have. Along with their hands upon me."

Her hesitancy, her subdued tone, now caused a feeling of dread to birth itself inside my chest. "But you do not like what you had need to tell me?"

"Not at all. But you seek justice in the killing of Master Brewster--you, your father and his fishing admirals, do you not?"

"This has become common knowledge, has it?"

"It has. Along with much fear and conjecture."

"Which we work to dispel," I sought to assure her.

"Aye. And so I must tell you."

I leaned closer. "What is it, Abby?"

"On St. John's Eve. I found something that had been buried on my master's land, near the cliffs. The spring rains must have revealed enough for me to see the glint of silver."

"Silver?"

It was a pair of pantaloons, with four silver buttons. Buttons that fastened nothing, that were sewn only for decoration. Only three of the four buttons remained, Charlotte. The missing place showed signs it had been torn free. I remembered those pantaloons. They had once belonged to Captain Dunbar, but he'd given them to Primus, as he often did to keep his man the best dressed servant on the island. He made a great show of his 'silver studded manservant' is what I recall."

I fought the notion of Primus hastening a man to his death. "Yet others wear silver buttons."

"But these matched the one on your mantle shelf, Charlotte. It's the one retrieved from the hand of the dead man, is it not? That's what I was rowing over to tell you. Show you."

"Where are the pantaloons now?"

"They were in the boat with me. They must have been washed out to sea when it capsized."

Primus. Now escaped from his lifelong indenture. Living with his beloved Asson and the Beothuk. Randall and I both felt sure of this, though none of the Beothuk or the Mi'kmaq, not even my own grandmothers, had confirmed it was so. Primus, who had once shared his Bermuda stories with Randall and me. Did he murder Master Brewster? Why? Did the servant hate his peacemaker master so much as to thwart his ambitions to impress his countess with harmony around her improved estate? Captain Dunbar had stolen any hope of Primus achieving his own freedom. That knowledge had changed, perhaps embittered our fishing companion. But did it make him a murderer?

The silence was heavy between myself and my friend.

"Charlotte," Abby whispered. "This is a painful restoration of memory. Primus never did me any harm."

"Nor I."

"At least I do not believe it was he under that Stag's head."

"Why not?"

"Because I also remember a hand. Grasping my wrist in the boat that night. It was a pale hand."

"Ah."

Well, that was something. Randall and I did not help the someone who tried to murder our friend to escape, at least.

Abigail sighed. "I suppose we must tell your father."

"Yes. We must tell him everything. He will have thoughts, and conjectures. If Primus is Beothuk now, they will not give him up for a trial, for judgement—here or in England. My father must know. He will help us avoid a war between us and my grandmother's people.

"Please, God," Abby whispered.

Papa's reaction to our news was careful and considered. "There is nothing physical to show those who may sit in judgement," he explained. "You are female, under the age of majority, and a servant, Abby. As a witness, this all weighs against you in this imperfect world. I am glad you remembered these things. It adds to our knowledge, our search. But it need not be exposed to any but us at present. Let me take up this burden."

Abby and I looked to each other and nodded.

"Here is a thought," Papa added. "Just because his pantaloons were buried near the place Master Brewster went over the cliff, it does not prove that Primus was in them at the time of the murder."

Slow smiles crept over our faces. Of course. That was true. And another thought visited. Those pantaloons could have been buried there after the town surmised that we were hunting for a murderer.

My father stroked his ear ornament. "The fact remains, that someone sought to harm you, Abby, most likely for the knowledge you were bringing to us that night. You have been safe with us since. That someone must not discover that your memory has been restored. Another reason to keep the knowledge among the three of us only."

Aye, sir," Abigail and I said together, as unburdened shipmates of our captain.

But our captain did not have the esteem of every female in our household. Mary entered the kitchen later that day as my father was reading among Mr. Shakespeare's sonnets. Her face was dark with anger. "Do you think of me as a child? Is that why you sought to keep me ignorant? Those people being judged, killed! They were our neighbors!"

My father closed his collection. "I know, dear heart."

"You do not trust me."

"It was not a matter of trust, Mary, but of finding the right time, the right words."

"By studying that playwright and not our bible? It is always the right time for the truth, sir."

She turned on her heel and left the house again. I made to follow, but Papa stayed my hand. "Let her be for now, Charlotte. We cannot understand the nature of her grief. Perhaps she needs to be alone with it."

"But she has not been alone in St. John's before. She may not find her way back."

"Someone will show her if she loses her way. Mayhap she needs this brief flight from our household. To think for herself. She will find her way back."

"Of course," I said, trying to convince myself.

And she did, before dark, easing my heart. Abby opened the scullery door to her. Cousin Mary seemed stronger, and more serene. Perhaps she'd found God's grace in the beauties of our high summer day.

But we all suffered from troubled minds.

I talked over Mary's reaction with Randall. "How is it that the Salem news has traveled this fast?" I asked him. "That she learned it before Papa was able to find the right words?"

Randall laid down his bell. "The notorious travels faster than the good. More ships are in the harbor now from the colonies. And the trials and their details are the talk of all. But, I agree, it is baffling. The townspeople don't reach out to Mary, as a rule. Her imperious nature is a little off-putting."

"A little?"

Even in times of strife, our Randall could make me smile.

That was the beginning of Mary's walks. One who had always kept her brothers close became solitary for stretches of time. One who had been reluctant to travel far from our house, from our few town-bound acres, now ventured out on her own, with no request of company.

She answered our inquiries with curt replies about finding her way about the town and shore. Did we not trust in her ability to locate her own way home? Sometimes she came in with muddy skirts, or a pretty shell for William, but otherwise we had no clues of where she went.

"Mh-m, Mary is nothing if not a purposeful lass," Randall commented on her changed behavior. "Should I follow her and see what pulls her from hearth and home?" he asked.

"Why...no, of course not," I objected, trying to convince myself as well as he. "Mary is so touchy about our trust as it is. And her walks seem to be doing her good. Perhaps she has made herself a friend. A friend who is having a good influence over her. She works by my side in the kitchen now. She asks many questions about my remedies, what knowledge I am gaining about meals, and the nature and prosperity of our business. She has even helped me present our goods to our purchasers and traders with a cordial smile."

But although she seemed changed in our household and towards me, her animosity toward my father intensified. When he discovered a Boston newspaper in her basket after one of her seaside excursions, she held on until the paper ripped between them. I stood outside the doorway, watching.

"Who gave you this?" he asked.

"You have no right! You hold no dominion over me."

"Mary. Allow me to read the account first."

"So you can lie about it?"

"So we can talk about it. Decide how much to tell your brothers."

"Hiding is only for babies like William," she claimed. "Not for me. I am almost Charlotte's age."

"Forgive me, Mary, but you are not."

"Why? Because I cannot speak to the Indians? Find roots and fungus and strange plants with properties to heal? Mayhap to harm? Keep accounts? Plant stubby, misshapen corn? Or climb the rigging of your ship like a man?"

My father was stunned into silence. I entered the room, reached out my hand to our cousin, but she shrank away. "You hate me!" she proclaimed. "I try so hard to understand you, but you hate me. For taking up your duties as the woman of this house. For being of the Covenant."

"No, Mary."

"There is no hate in this house," my father said quietly.

She wiped an errant tear away with the back of her hand and stepped back from us both. "Are you part of their plan?"

"Plan?" my father echoed.

"Whose plan?" I added.

"Is that why you will not bring our parents to us? Or us to them?"

My father sighed. "Mary, your father's wish—"

"What do you know of my father's wishes? He will not even write to you. They have hanged our last minister! The satanic infection has spread to Amesbury and Marblehead and Connecticut. Perhaps to here? Are you and Charlotte part of it? Are we in the hands of our enemies? This is a place of mists and wild, godless people who dance around bonfires and call yellow birds to my brother's finger!"

We stared at her, confounded.

She gasped, then began wringing her hands. "I have spoken too much, too much."

"You have spoken ideas that are not your own," my father said sternly. "Whose are they?"

She did not answer, only climbed the back stairs, and shut the door of the female part of the house.

"Go to Randall," my father instructed me. "Have him follow her on her next walking excursion. Someone is taking advantage of this child's grief. Someone is poisoning her mind."

I left right away for Randall's dwelling, where he was working on a beautiful, misty rendering of Manley's Cove in summer. He wiped his brush clean of the blue pigment he'd mixed from Papa's homecoming gift. "Well, he's come around to providing a closer watch on the contrary Mistress Mary, has he?" My friend voiced his relief and ready to take over his watchman duties.

But for a time, Mary's excursions ceased, as quickly as they had begun. Randall's abilities did not seem to be needed after all.

Until they began again.

We were ready.

Chapter 23
Spell Song

It began on a Monday in mid-September, when even the pleasant days seemed like the good-bye of summer once we were in the shade. It was the start of a different pattern for our family. Because of the war and our obligations toward our English family cousins, Papa would not cross the Atlantic, and I would not be going inland to my grandmothers for the winter season.

Once the decision was reached, we became busy making the house- which we usually shut down- more snug for the winter. Our overwintering shore families had made it clear that the winds off the water made for harsher weather than I was used to inland. And my poor papa was used to visiting lands of palms, dates, olives, and oranges in winter.

William toddled after me with my buckets of chinking mud, resplendent in his new blue wool trousers. Abigail had taken up his baby dress six inches so that, combined with the trousers, he now looked like a miniature yeoman farmer. The stiches were carefully made, but wide, so that they could be easily removed as it returned to its former purpose, should another baby enter the family.

I was trying mightily to be accepting of losing my beautiful story-telling time with my Mi'kmaq and Beothuk relatives. I would miss them. I had so much more to learn from the healing ways of my grandmothers, especially as Rose Brewster's time grew nearer. The brothers Sam and Gideon had worked to restore their own fishing stations and houses. They left her and Mrs. Gavin to run Raven Hill.

I made up the teas I'd learned from my grandmothers. Once her first three months' sickness was past, Rose no longer needed the sarsaparilla tonic to stimulate her appetite. I crushed blue violet plants and mixed them with lambs' fat as a salve for the expanding middle. She bloomed nicely and even seemed content with facing her widowed motherhood, although she asked me with every visit whether there was any sign she was going to greet her heart's desire—a daughter. I would laugh and assure her there was no way to know for sure, and that we would all learn on the babe's birthday.

Mrs. Gavin's housekeeping duties expanded to running the whole estate, and by all accounts the predictions of it going to ruin were not proving true. Mrs. Gavin had even increased her cattle herd.

Their neighbor Captain Dunbar seemed most pleased of all. On one of my visits I came across him in Raven Hill's north pasture with his own work crew, helping to expand her pasture for more cattle. "And more butter," he reminded me. "My countess will be so pleased to have such butter, from such neighbors," he assured both women, with a wave of his plumed hat to us all.

Rose watched him go. "My new widow's life seemsto have a good effect on all, even the man who thought me fit only for a convent," she observed.

"Oh you, too?" I asked.

Mrs. Gavin laughed with us. "I think the good captain wants to burden the poor nuns with the lot of us troublesome women!"

I only knew the Beothuk and Mi'kmaq ways of a woman's labor and birth and had not witnessed the process among my father's people. Mrs. Gavin was a godsend. She promised to attend Rose with me. She had done so with friends and relatives over her longer life. "This has been a most enjoyable time for my mistress, despite her circumstances," she confided quietly. "You and the children under your care have been so good for us both over these months. I think our Rose is looking forward to her new station in life with more hope."

That was important, according to my grandmothers. Being in balance and with an open heart was good for a woman entering this powerful, important time. And with Gideon and Sam and their objections to her inheritance keeping away, perhaps she felt her home secure under her feet.

"But even in the good company of Phillip and Will, I worry that she still seems heart-set on having a daughter," I admitted to Mrs. Gavin.

"Aye, true. But I think that has more to do with providing less threat to Master Brewster's elder sons and their place here in our community."

"But should she reject her baby—"

"It is not time to worry, Charlotte," she told me, "about my young mistress. Or about your own ability to see her through her birth and lying-in. You are young, aye, but have steady hands and a calm nature. And your friendship with Rose is restored, which is what my young mistress needed. She is thriving now. And when her time comes, we will be there to encourage and assist. Besides, 'tis the mother and babe have the real work," she declared. "Nature will have its course. We are but there to ease the way as best we can."

That seemed a philosophy in keeping with what I'd observed among the Beothuk and Mi'kmaq births I had witnessed over my two winters in training with my grandmothers. The birthing mothers welcomed us into their homes. We all spoke in quiet tones, supported each woman's steps, her arms, her wishes as she ushered new life into the world.

The thought of those wondrous birthing times brought the soft music of a Mi'kmaq lullaby from my throat as I chinked the wall of our dining hall around the fireplace. William's little fingers, so busy with the pies he was making from the mud I'd provided him, stilled. Then his eyelashes fluttered, then drooped. Finally, he curled into my draping skirts and was still. I smiled. The song had done its work.

"What do the words mean?" Mary asked from the doorway.

"What the words of all lullabies mean," I answered, smiling. "Put your head down, go to sleep, little one."

"It sounded like you were casting a spell."

"All lullabies are spell songs, cousin. Luring children to their rest."

"You make it sound benign."

"I believe it is benign. And that lullabies are based in love and good caretaking."

She walked into the room. "Shall I move him to his bed?"

"Oh no. He is so peaceful there. And he has left me room to maneuver. I think I can finish without disturbing him."

"May I sit here by the window then, where the light is best for my stitches?" she asked quietly as she moved around her sleeping brother.

"Of course. I should like your company." I took a cloth from my apron pocket. "And to

210

appreciate something finer than this mess I have made around the hearth."

She brought out the two-ply woolen yarn on linen embroidery cushion she had been working on as a gift to her mother. I admired her skill and the beauty of her design, even as I cleared some of my own muddy concoction off the side of my face.

We worked on each of our tasks for a while in silence.

"Will I ever have answers to all my questions?" she asked suddenly.

I sat back, remembering myself at her tumultuous time of life, between the worlds of child and adult. I was there still, of course, but being pushed by my circumstances to act more in one world than the other. But I remembered well that feeling of being both and neither, a strange creature, fitting nowhere. "I often feel overwhelmed and wonder the same, Mary. But now I think the questions are more important."

"More important?"

"Aye. Being curious. Wanting to know. About things large and small. About the wars that are dividing us. How are we to find our way back to the ways of peace, of friendship, of sharing knowledge and trading goods."

That frown appeared again. "It is not our place to think upon such things. That is the domain of our fathers, brothers, and husbands."

"Do we not live in the world with them? Will we not suffer beside them if we cannot find our way to peace?"

She stopped working at her sewing. "Do you find answers to your questions in your book of Shakespeare? In your time with the Indians?"

I smiled. Was I getting used to Mary's challenges? "I look to both for guidance," I answered her. "But both Mr. Shakespeare and my grandmothers ponder yet more questions, I'm afraid."

She glanced at another volume--the book we now read aloud most often. It was in its revered place. "The Bible provides answers," she declared firmly.

"Many have found guidance in those pages, yes. But our Lord Jesus asks many questions himself, does he not?"

"What questions?"

"Well, here is one. 'Which now of these three, thinkest thou, was neighbor unto him that fell among the thieves?'"

"The Good Samaritan! I like that story!"

"Oh, so do I. What about: 'Which of you by taking thought can add one cubit unto his stature?'"

A smile lit Mary's face. "My father quotes that one to my mother when he says she worries too much!"

"And my father to me. Those two men must be related to each other, yes?"

We laughed quietly then. At last. Something to make us laugh together, other than the antics of our beloved William. I offered thanks for this moment in my heart.

I ventured further. "Jesus pokes and prods us to think about important things with his questions, I think. To fortify a great blessing, our free will."

Mary looked down at her sleeping brother, who had pulled up my skirts about him like a blanket. "One of our neighbors in Salem, an elder woman called Rebecca Nurse; al her children lived. Lived into their adult years and started families themselves. People whispered about it, thought it unnatural, when all other families suffered losses."

"Did they?"

"Is that why they killed her? Is that why they thought she was in league with the Devil? Because her children lived, and theirs did not?"

A terrible cold replaced the joy in my heart. "I do not know, Mary." How had Mary acquired knowledge of the circumstances of this woman, I wondered? Randall said there were newspaper accounts of the trials discussed deep in the night around men at the tavern. But Mary would have been noticed among that company.

My cousin looked up from her stitches. "The judges of Salem. They have free will, this great blessing, as you see it. How does it work for them to decide to kill Rebecca Nurse? A pious woman with children and grandchildren? And why did they come after my parents? They lost babies, the same as others. My father is not of the covenant, but my mother is, and they have been good and generous to our neighbors, and the poor. Why, Charlotte?"

"These are good questions," was all I could think of saying.

Chapter 24
The Mummer Stag Revealed

I loved walking along the cliffs in the September mist, after my visits with Rose and Mrs. Gavin at Raven Hill. The air is so heavy with the salt spray of the ocean beyond that I feel among the waves again, and close to my mother. But that day, out of the mists, came George Wyatt and the Widow Attley, pulling me out of the thoughts of Cousin Mary's questions, distant silences, and melancholy turns of mind.

"Well met," I greeted the couple.

"I thought we might find you up here," Constance Attley declared, catching her breath. "This man is finally ready to make a full accounting of his suit against you."

The man in question stood before me, his hat in his hand.

I nodded. "Master Wyatt. What is there left to be said between us on this matter?"

"Go on, my man", she prodded.

George Wyatt brought the hat back to his head, then looked at his empty hands. "Captain Dunbar put me up to making the formal complaint against you."

"How so?" I asked.

"I had my suspicion against you, mind, blighted soul that I be. But Captain Dunbar convinced me it was my obligation to enter them into the court."

"Captain Dunbar? Our new peacemaker? The good neighbor to the women of Raven Hill?" I teased him on the merchant's changed disposition.

"Oh, that is how he prefers others to think of him, now, aye, Mistress. At first, I thought his scheme to set me against you was because he was angry that your father came with such speed to port that he was made Fishing Admiral ahead of him."

"That was not the reason?"

"Not the whole of it, I'm thinking."

What was the source of the hesitancy in the man so full of words when it came to his lady love? "Why else then would Captain Dunbar urge you to press your suit against me?

"My land, lady. He has always wanted it, as he seeks to control the world around for himself, to bring his titled betrothed to these shores. I did not abandon my place. I sold it."

"Did you?"

"To Captain Dunbar."

"I see."

"For a price I would only receive if I kept the buyer a secret, said he. So now the price is forfeit." He shrugged. "It was a promissory note only anyways. Who has coin in any of the colonies? It is how he is seeking the whole of the cliffs above St. John's, you see.

He knows it is illegal to own land, except through the grants given to the first families. It is why he settles Sam and Gideon's accounts at the tavern, pays to rebuild and supply their fishing stations, hires workers to expand Mrs. Gavin's dairy. He does none of it from neighborly concern. He wants that mansion house, that land—all of it. I was just a small cog to get rid of. But the Brewsters have the stone house—the grandest mansion house of St. John's, built in the time of the first Lord Baltimore's settlement. Captain Dunbar-, he seeks to grant it to his lady love. And she is coming. Expecting it, says he. I fear for what he might do to those doltish sons, to that little ladybird of a widow. He has grand ambitions, has Captain Dunbar."

"Yes," I agreed. "My father and I know something of them."

"Do not get drawn in! I am fortunate. I hope to soon be in the arms of this woman- a woman I will never deserve. I am but a poor farmer, and no great danger to him now. You and your father are merchants, like him. He can do you more harm. And has tried to harm you, through me."

He looked to the hard gaze of his betrothed. She nodded, then took me by the arm. "We must look after each other, Charlotte Jaddore" she said. "Tell your father of this. And heed the words of this poor blighted fool of a man."

I felt shaken, as I had on the night Captain Dunbar drank cognac with my father. Why did Captain Dunbar hold such personal enmity toward me? Was it that my father's love for me was keeping him from joining in his schemes, his pursuits of greater wealth in the slave trade with Africa? Or was his greed wider?

It was time to visit Randall. To bring him to Papa. To go over this new knowledge attained, courtesy of the Widow Attley, who I think was finally ready to be Farmer Wyatt's wife now that the full truth of the witch accusation against me was revealed.

But Randall and I have a lovely bond, a sense of when one needs another. So I discovered him coming to me on the path to his dwelling. He grabbed my hand. "Raise your hood, little sister."

I did as he commanded.

"Good. Come."

Using his hold on me instead of his walking stick, we made fast progress toward St. John's portside, where he whistled. Seaman Henson, of my father's crewmen appeared from the shadows and brought us to a launch boat. We got on board, and he rowed us out of the harbor.

The stars were coming out in the night sky when we rounded the curve that led to Manley's Cove. Anchored there was my father's ship.

I broke our silence. "Why are we rowing out to the *Esperance*?" I asked Randall.

"All will be illuminated," he said as we reached the side. We were hailed and welcomed aboard by the night watchman, First Mate Tomlinson.

Randall led me to the main deck behind the mizzenmast. Approaching one of the boats from the deck of the *Esperance*, he drew away a sail, waiting to be mended. Under it, sat the great antlered head of the Mummer's Stag.

And a voice, from above us. "I placed it in Captain Worthing's skiff that night, Wavewalker."

I looked up into the clear-eyed stare of Darting Badger. "You did? Why?"

He shrugged. "I find your father's people... interesting."

"You are the Stag Mummer?"

"Yes." His shoulders sagged. "Even after warnings from the clan mothers who kept my secret, even from you. I wanted to study the strange ones. Not as myself, their trading partner, now suspected of working for the French, their enemies. But from the inside. What better time, what more harmless way than using one of their feasting days? When I learned of the masked, disguised ones, the Mummers, I thought it would be a good thing to become one. None guessed it was me under the stag's head, so I was not found out that night. I thought it a great success—"

"In spying."

"Diplomacy," he corrected me, "I was on a good road, Wavewalker. One leading to understanding. Of your strange world, even when they played at it being built in the opposite, contrary way. Then came the fire.”

“At the fishing stations of the Brewster brothers. You were there,” I realized. “That is why you gave such an accurate accounting of it at the trial. Adding to the remembering of those frightened boys and the stumbling mummers. It was you—seeing all yourself!”

“Singed my antlers dragging those useless brothers to the shore,” he admitted with disgust.

Randall stepped between us “After the murder of Brewster,” he continued, “and then Abigail Barrie’s clobbering, the Mummer Stag became suspected of causing all the evil that has befallen us over the past few months.”

“I could not tell then,” Darting Badger maintained.

I frowned, considering. “But you had a say in the Fishing Admirals’ court. Your words were respected.”

“When I had a peacekeeper’s place. And outsider to both, called upon by our kin the Beothuk, to keep the boys safe from Englishmen’s wrath.”

“The grandmothers,” I realized now. “They were doing more than weaving atonement baskets.”

Darting Badger sighed. “They might want my head in one of those baskets now, for seeking a place inside the Englishmen’s world,” he admitted.

Randall linked himself to both of us when he placed hands on our shoulders. "We must keep his secret, Charlotte. Our friend will be suspected of murder, by real or spectral means," he explained. "You know where this can lead."

I did indeed. "But how did Abigail Barrie think she saw you on St. John's Eve?"

"She did see me. I was there when Captain Worthing put her in that boat. I was keen to come dancing around the bonfire, I thought to show all the harmless Stag Mummer. That the mysterious one who they did not guess was me, now come to dance with them. She must have seen my shadow. But someone else was in that boat with her. Someone else hit her and shoved her in, hoping the waves would take her."

"And why did they not?" I asked him pointedly.

"Well. I am a good swimmer, as are all island Mi'kmaq. I knew if I could get her to shore, others would care for her."

"You were her sea monster. You wreathed her in seaweed, bladder kelp with air pockets to float her ashore. You saved her, just as you saved the Brewster brothers from the fire."

He drew his hand over the shaved half of his head. "Huh. English people find trouble for themselves on land and sea both," he said.

I considered what I had learned. Neither Primus nor Darting Badger sought to keep

Abigail Barrie from reaching me with what she'd found. And we had been looking in the wrong direction for the one who struck her down. And killed James Brewster. We had been entangled in a web of sea creatures and the Mummer stag, of burning fishing stations and spectral evidence. There was a simpler reason the master of Raven Hill was killed. By a very made-of-flesh murderer among us. And I was finally certain I knew who it was.

I had to find my father.

But then we saw the signal light flashes from the shore at Manely's Cove. I raised my spyglass and realized that the murderer had found us.

Chapter 25
Captivity

We had our own code of communication, my father and I, born from our years at sea-- a number code he had learned from a French admiral. The ship lamp's candlepower was enhanced by shards of a looking glass, so its signals could be seen better through the fog, and at longer distances. The code was simple and straightforward. I counted the blinking lights.

Danger.

We rowed ashore, found the lamp's candle was almost gutted. We raised ours higher. The scent of gunpowder and a trail of blood led away from the lamp.

"There is no way back to St. John's from here," Darting Badger said. "All trails lead to the barrens and the slope bogs, the land of the Beothuk."

Randall and I knew this. The crewmen looked to each other in dismay.

I placed my hand on Seaman Morgan's arm. "Row back to the ship," I instructed. "Return to St. John's. Tell the fishing admirals we fear Captain Jaddore has been abducted. Seek their guidance. Return."

"Reinforced, armed?"

"Aye." I agreed.

Seaman Morgan pulled his boarding axe from his belt and shoved it against Randall. "You've a good arm on ye, lad. Look after Young Charlotte."

When he tried to give Darting Badger his cutlass, he received a sneer.

Once we helped to push them off, Randall, Darting Badger and I turned to our task, raising our own lanterns higher.

"They are still close," Darting Badger whispered. He disappeared behind a pine.

"Wait," Randall called out softly. "We should—"

And then all sign of him was gone.

I turned a full circle in place. Silently, as I was taught by my Beothuk relatives. But then, a soft blow and darkness descended.

I heard flowing creek water. Close. Almost at my feet. Rope-bound feet, their tether extending to hands, also bound together before me. A leash was tied round a black spruce tree. I had traveled up from the bay, then. How? My only comfort was the lemon and salt sea scent of my father beside me. And something more deadly: gunpowder.

Out of the darkness came the voice I expected. "Make the bleeding stop, healer. I have things to say to both of you before you die."

Then footfalls, away from us.

My eyes adjusted further to the starless, moonless night. I forced my terrified mind to move closer to my father's still form. Breathing, yes. He was breathing. Then, to work. I focused my attention on the left side of his face, the gunpowder's burn, the flowing blood. Grateful my hands were bound loosely before me, I was able to use them to rip up the seam of my linen underskirt until it was clear of its muddied hem. I tore off two clean sections. I then crawled toward the creek bed, doused both in the water, and returned to my father's side. I held the first cloth firmly against my father's head wound.

"Papa," I coaxed. "Open your eyes."

His dear voice rose up from the darkness. "The signal was to my ship."

"And I was on it."

A sigh, now. "Of course you were."

His eyelids flickered.

"Drink," I urged. "Restore yourself. Drink."

I squeezed drops from the second cloth into his mouth. I saw he was not restrained, nor was he tied to the tree. Not considered a threat, then.

He took in a shuddering breath. "Thought he'd killed me with that prized flintlock pistol of his. Thought he'd have nothing to lure you here with." A small laugh escaped his lips before his whisper softened even more. "You did not come alone?"

"With Randall and Darting Badger. Papa, I fear he has killed them."

"Those two? Not likely. And the hired crewmen he enlisted in his hunt of us looked ready to bolt even before he brought me down. Courage. We must keep him talking, *Petite Onde*. We must keep ourselves alive until our help, it arrives."

"Yes, Papa."

His head dropped to my shoulder. I looked up as the sneering form of Captain Dunbar returned. His silver-studded carriage pistols were on full display tucked into the red sash around his middle. He was wise to restrain me. I wanted to kill him.

Yes. He had much to say. "I guessed Primus was coming here, your fishing spot from years gone by. So I wound my timbering trails in this direction. As I was ready to pounce, he disappeared. Your miserable Fishing Court proved useless in finding him—my property! Stolen from me by you!""

My father's head rose from my shoulder. "Primus stole himself, I think, sir."

"Ah, still life in you, Martin Jaddore? I tried to be peaceable, did I not? I offered you a partnership in my ventures. I gave you good advice. A chance to avoid all this."

"What are you talking about?"

"Our future together! But did you take heed? No. You were blinded by your affection for this... this mistake of yours."

I felt my father's back stiffen in fury. I touched it with my fingers, then my palm, hoping it was urging him to stay calm, and think clearly. And keep Captain Dunbar with his loaded pistols talking, as our lives may depend upon it.

Papa patted my hand before he spoke, but the anger was still laced in his even tone. "The mistake I made was in thinking you had changed, had become a peacemaker."

"Oh, but I am exactly that, sir! For the Brewsters and beyond! There will be no peace on this island until everyone knows his place. Your own bewitched charge who came out of Salem is correct. God smiles on the elect. Proper order must be maintained---witches, Indians, Quakers, upstart servants, and women must be rooted out if they know not their place in God's order. Surely it is the devil's work, women thinking they have the means to lord it over men! I thought I had them convinced you killed their father. Thad! Ezra! Where the devil are you?" he called out.

Crewmen. Perhaps my father was right, and they'd had a change of heart.

Captain Dunbar looked eastward. "My esteemed Countess will find that out soon enough. We will marry, she will abide with me at her place here on my island. I will build battlements. I will help conquer France and their filthy native allies both. I will bring glory to my name and achieve my own title. That fool Phips is not the only one who can get himself a knighthood from that German-born King! Avalon will not be ruled by soft-hearted fishing admirals, but by a royal governor, who appoints royal justices to do his bidding. My bidding. I will restore order by way of the sword. My sword!"

He pulled it from its scabbard, approached us. I drew my bound hands up before my father's form.

"Charlotte, no!" he admonished me as the sword cut through my sleeve instead of its target. I caught the scent of strong drink as our tormentor stumbled against us. Something else happened too, though I felt rather than saw it. With his quick wit and unbound hands, my father caught hold of a pistol.

Captain Dunbar stumbled back from us, then laughed. He moved in closer. With more care he held the tip of his sword to my father's chin, "Understand me, Jerseyman?"

My father kept his head high. Crusted blood had sealed his left eyelid closed. "Too late, yes, I do."

Our attacker stepped back, lowered his sword, but did not replace it to its scabbard. Yes. He had but one pistol in his sash now. I adjusted my skirts to cover my father's catch of the other, though I did not dare to look down.

"Charlotte, your arm."

"A scratch," I whispered, assuring the worry in his eyes over my injury.

Josiah Dunbar continued his rant. "My Countess is coming...expecting a grand mansion house, vast acreage, the empire of my making that I promised her. I could not wait for that dithering family to come around to my way of thinking, to settle their debts with what I needed: their house and land. And then that love-struck Brewster complicated things further with a new wife, a new family started. Oh, the things that go on when I am ploughing the seas, looking after my beloved's holdings in Bermuda!

"Well, the sons were hardly a match for me," he continued, slashing the night air with his sword. "If I could just cut the family off at its head. I would have bought out the rest, after their father's fall—even the share of that conniving servant girl. If not you and your curiosity! An old man falls off a cliffside, what could be a more natural death?" He turned on his heel and faced us again. "But no, Jaddore! Your daughter had to find him before the tide came in, washing him out to sea and off my hands!"

He began to pace before us. My father shifted, making the pistol disappear behind his back. He had only one good eye, and me with my bound hands, what chance did we have?

"We might not wash out to sea so easily either," my father said mildly.

The pacing stopped. "It matters not--I can wait no longer. I have received word. My countess is coming! Her tone is imperious, displeased, imagine! After all I have done for her! She must see the fine work I have made of her trust, her fortune, the power of her name. You will not stand in my way, you, or your witch of a daughter, who I have made sure will be blamed for all that is to come."

"What is to come?" I asked, trying to match the coolness in my father's tone and failing miserably at the ambition.

Still, Captain Dunbar closed in on us slowly, smiling. "Only the poisoning of a whole family—the Brewster family- by way of one of your Red Indian mushroom stews. Ah yes, I've put more than mountain ash in their tonic, you witch! I have learned all your concoctions from your little Puritan apprentice. Such a fearful, wretched child is Mary English, separated from her pious people. Not trusting your father because he can only remember benign New Testament passages of the merciful Jesus, and not the plagues, the prophets, and the angry God she is more accustomed to hearing about from her Salem minister."

"All of which you provided her," my father said as we both now knew the identity of my cousin's secret friend.

"Oh, aye, Martin! Mistress Mary found, if not the father she seeks, a doting uncle in me. I provided her with cakes and company at our little hidden alley table outside my fishing station. I was happy to listen to her prattle, as long as I learned what was needed to bring you down, Charlotte Jaddore. A heady compound of poison mushrooms you so ably described should ease all the Brewster family sufferings forever. I shall bring it to them myself, with your urging to finish every drop.

"They are in my debt, so I shall take over their house and land upon their demise. I will allow the town to put you to your death for the poisoning—a woman's crime, is it not? Quickly, in their anger, their rage, without a trial or being sent to London in chains. For I feel sure they will be mortified after treating you with honor for so long. Honor betrayed. I have seen such rage, leading to massacres of whole families of your red-skinned savages. I know how to fan the flames. And I will. Yours will be a quick, but not an easy death."

I held my head high. "None will believe you."

"They will not have to. They will have the witness account of your own Salem relative. They know how to accuse, those New Englanders, they are full of a fine and righteous indignation. All my kindness toward your cousin will be called upon."

"You have shown me no kindness, sir."

I recognized the small, lonely voice coming out of the darkness.

"Oh, Mary," I breathed out.

A nervous laugh burst from our oppressor. "Why. Fair Mistress English. You were to watch over our prisoners along with my crew."

"They are dispatched."

Randall appeared, flipping the boarding axe as if it was his crier bell. "Into the woods. And we talked her into following you here, sir." Darting Badger claimed a place beside Mary. "And listening for herself," he said, as he cut my leash with a single slice of his wife's knife. "Never leave an Irishman captive's mouth unbound," he counseled our oppressor.

My heart took a leap at seeing my companions in such good health and humor.

Captain Dunbar's own loquaciousness was at an end. He reached into his sash, discovered that one of his pistols was missing, then fumbled but found the remaining one. He pointed it squarely at me as its flint stuck spark and a shot rang out.

I raised my still-bound hands to my face, closed my eyes, and said a prayer to St. Anne.

Chapter 26
Caribou Justice

That was how I missed seeing the pistol flying from his hand.

"Good shot, sir," Randall complimented my father.

Captain Dunbar stared at his missing fingers, before his good hand took hold of his sword. He made a flying leap that began his run into the darkness of the woods beyond us.

Darting Badger looked me over as he finished releasing me from my bonds. Randall and Mary helped my father rise to his feet.

"Cousins, can you forgive me?" Mary asked.

My father smiled. "Well, your part in saving our lives is good atonement."

"But we must warn the Brewsters—" I cried.

"No need. I told him the mushrooms you hung high on the hearth held poison. It was those he took. It was not the truth I told."

She raised her remorse-filled eyes to mine, but there was no time for words between us.

"Are you able to track?" Darting Badger asked my father and me, the weakest members of his hunting party.

I looked to Papa. We nodded our willingness together and linked arms. I could help his sight and he could provide me the strength of an extra arm.

Dawn's light was growing over the eastern horizon. We entered the land of the Beothuk. I heard clicking. Only one animal made that sound—the caribou.

They were migrating from the barren lands of the northern peninsula to the mixed forests of Avalon. And it was mating season, with males making thunderous noise as their antlers engaged, clashed as they fought for dominance. The Beothuk followed, and now watched from their places in and among the trees. Further down the valley, I imagine they had prepared birch barriers for a more directed hunt. It would be a good, plentiful winter if the hunt went well.

For now we watched in awe as Captain Dunbar stumbled into their midst. I had never seen so many of the powerful caribou, plump from a summer of grazing. Captain Dunbar ran, but there was no keeping up with their power. One, a great antlered male, spotted him by the glint of his desperately raised sword. The stag made of the man a target. He lowered his head, charged. He gored Captain Dunbar, who kept shouting, kept whacking at the animal's head without making a mark. At the cliffside the stag raised his great head, still containing the wildly flailing man, and tossed him over the edge.

Captain Dunbar disappeared into the bog below.

My father's diminished strength finally gave out. He sank to his knees beside me. Two tall, red-ochred Beothuk warriors appeared, wearing beaver skins and trembling ash branches, looking like shape-shifting jenu, the supernatural guardian beings said to inhabit the dense forests of Newfoundland. They leaned down and placed their shoulders to either side of my father, raising him back to his feet. One was Asson's brother, Ishu.

The other was Primus.

The wind stirred my skirts. "I have never seen the caribou come so close to Manely's Cove before," I whispered.

"Well, we might have nudged them," Primus said, flexing those strong arms.

Darting Badger joined him and Ishu. "A bit," he agreed.

"Loved by the Waves," Ishu addressed me formally in slowly intoned Beothuk, "I think our relations among the caribou agreed to protect you from the evil in the mist of your own. The ones who take too much."

My father extended his arm to each of the Beothuk who had revealed themselves to us. They took his friendship offering in various degrees of wariness, it seemed to me. "Have your daughter look after you and that arm, Captain," Primus suggested, before he followed the other hunter warriors after the thundering herd.

Chapter 27
The Countess Arrives

With her hoisted skirts, windswept hair blowing out of a bejeweled turban, and keen eyes scanning the horizon, she looked more like a pirate queen than a countess. My father took her hand as she stepped off the gangplank- his fishing admirals, and her retinue a respectful distance behind them.

The crowd gathered at the dock and parted.

I wore my grey gown. Standing beside me, Abigail Barrie let out a sigh. "They make a splendid couple, do your father and the countess."

"Now, Abby, papa is acting in his official duty as Fishing Admiral," I reminded her.

"Ah, but still. He is great friends with the beloved woman of the King of France, your godmother. Why should he not count an English Countess among his admirers?"

I was forced to admit they did look matched, each a bit wilder than was to be expected, even here in Newfoundland. And her wide smile told me the beautiful countess would not have objected to Abby's assessment.

But my most fond remembrance of them came not at that moment. Or in the day's welcoming ceremonies, or her visit to her holdings at Adlington Manor, where she only retired to rest each day, preferring to visit fishing stations and the homes of folk. All were happy to receive her gracious self, especially after thinking of her as a haughty queen who would come to lord over us all. Instead came a bright and curious lady, who learned games from our children and how to render salt with the men. She loved visiting Randall too, and the places of the scenes he'd painted. She even sat for a portrait of herself. For all, she'd depended on my father as her guide.

My fondest remembrance came on one of the evenings in her company at our home, after my father's fellow fishing admirals and the countess's own retinue had left. All but one—her personal attendant lady's maid, who was enjoying the company of Abby Barrie and the English children around the hearth of our kitchen, where good scents soon emanated. Her mistress and Papa now sat in spindle-backed armchairs on either side of our hearth fire, like a long-married couple, talking over their day together, as I lit beeswax candles in our tin wall sconces to aid the hearth fire's illumination.

"I fear you will find no mourners for Captain Dunbar, Madame," he said gently.

"And after learning all that he has put this settlement through, I am not surprised."

Her gracious smile was gone, a thoughtful and compassionate countenance taking its place. "There has been a great deception," Countess Amelia continued. "Captain Dunbar was the overseer of my Bermuda holdings. He wrote to me about the investments he'd made, and his new scheme concerning my holdings in the fishing trade of the Avalon peninsula. And how he was preparing a home for me here."

"You were not betrothed?"

"I have never laid eyes on the man, and knew him only through our correspondence, which was never intimate, except, perhaps, in his own imagination. He never asked for my hand. And if he had, I would not have considered his offer. I am a countess by birth, inherited from my father who is from a family granted female access to title since the first Earl died leaving daughters in 1348. There have been many of us since. We marry late, in no need of any marriage bargain, as I have explained to countless suitors over my thirty years on God's green earth. I am most grievously distressed to see the havoc this man and his corrupt dreams have caused here."

My father and I shared relieved glances. "None of it was of your doing, Madame," he said.

She sipped from her glass of cognac. "But it was done in my name. In the name of my family," she said with sorrow lacing the cadences of her beautiful voice. "Understand this. I have come, not with any intent to receive a grand house or marriage partner. But I came with a purpose, Captain. A purpose I kept from the knowledge of my ill-chosen overseer. I came to right a wrong. A wrong that Captain Dunbar has perpetrated on his manservant, known by the name Primus."

I made a study of my hands, then chanced a look at my father. I saw from the firm set of his jaw that he shared my conviction. Countess Amelia would never get Primus back to Bermuda, not while Papa, Randall, his Beothuk relatives, and I could stand in the way of it.

The countess sensed our sudden frostiness, I think, for she now reached over to touch my father's arm. "Do not misunderstand, dear Captain. I came to offer this young man my apology for what was done in my name concerning him."

My father's brow quirked up, his frostiness remaining. "And what was that, Madame?"

"He has been kept in an indentured state."

"A lifelong indenture," my father reminded her.

"Yes, so his mother has informed me."

"His mother?"

I approached them. "But we understood Primus to be without living parents."

A sly smile came over her features. "Ah. Then you do know something of this young man, Mistress Charlotte? *N'est ce pas, mon capitaine?*"

My father's growl was her reply.

She shook her head and the ringlets beside her face danced. "His mother has kindly attended to my personal needs in hair, dress and companionship since she learned a lie from my overseer- of the sea taking her family. I intend to grant her an annuity to live where she chooses in any of my holdings. Perhaps she will take over the tending of Adlington Manor. For my estate is responsible for a grief no mother should endure."

A woman came out of the shadows of our kitchen, where she had been preparing a plum duff since learning it was my father's favorite. Neatly attired in a claret-colored gown and wide white laced linen cap, collar and cuffs, she was about fifty years. Her lovely features were also marked by a longing I'd seen on the faces of other women who'd had seafaring family lives cut short. There was also a strength of arms and tilt of chin that struck me as familiar. Her light green eyes searched ours, beseeching. "They said son and husband were lost to the waves. Does my son live?"

My father and I exchanged glances. Yes, he had seen the resemblance, too. He smiled uneasily. "When last we saw him, he was well, Madame."

The countess took the woman's hand. "Captain Jaddore, Mistress Charlotte, this is

Nan Flynn, Mrs. Orando. She served out her indenture, before she wed a seaman from my father's ship *Blue Mist.* Her husband was a free man. Their son was born as free as his parents. Together, whilst lately in Bermuda after many years together in England, Mrs. Orando and I have dug into my estate manager's deceptions. We found the documents to prove all. With your help, I wish to make amends to a young man you have called Primus. His given name is Hugh Orando."

The next day we brought Nan Orando to the edge of the ash grove where we had met my grandmothers at berry picking time. Then we backed away. She began to sing in a haunting voice, a beautiful lilting lullaby.

Rop tú mo dítiu, rop tú mo daingen;
rop tú nom-thocba i n-áentaid n-aingel.

Rop tú cech maithius dom churp, dom anmain;
rop tú mo flaithius i n-nim 's i talmain.

Rop tussu t' áenur sainserc mo chride;
ní rop nech aile acht Airdrí nime.

Slowly, sifting past the branches on moccasin-clad feet, a figure emerged. His formal lace, silk jacket and breeches replaced by a buckskin coat, its fringes wicking away the rain, its waist cinched by a colorful finger-woven sash in the manner of the Mi'kmaq and their French allies. His head snapped forward for a full view of the singer.

His wary eyes changed, then filled with tears.

"Mama?" he whispered.

* * *

We were finally able to return our cousins to their family in the spring of 1693, a full year after they came to us. Their father traveled to St. John's aboard one of his trading vessels, *The Morning Star*. He was not the same man I'd met in Salem the year before. Philip English wore his suffering year heavily, especially around his eyes. All resemblance to my father was gone. Even his children, overjoyed at the reunion, saw it, I think. Little William pressed himself into the soft grey wool of my skirts, avoiding his father's outstretched arms. Philip was patient, and got on his knees before his small son, waiting. Finally, William let go of my hand.

"Papa?" he whispered.

"Yes, William."

He took one more look at me, before he raised his fingers before his father's face. "I three."

"Yes, you are, and how well the number sits upon you, my son." The two fell into a fond embrace.

Mary English did not accompany her husband on his mission to collect their children, for she was making their house a home again and awaiting the birth of the newest member of their family. We expressed our joy at the tidings. But our cousin's strained look intensified. "I thought to save her, do you understand?" he confided, as the children joined Randall in the kitchen, enjoying the maple sugared walnuts he'd brought for them. "The same way John Proctor's wife was saved, by her pregnancy."

He shook his head. "Not saved, no. But the pregnancy would give her more time. Time for them to come to their senses, after my death. But my Mary, she was a grieving mother, separated from her children, wondering if each day would be her last. We added another burden, another life depending on her ebbing strength. Was it wrong, what we did? Will it cost me my lady wife, do you think? What was I saying? Oh, yes. They found Elizabeth Proctor guilty. They had the scaffold built and ready for her once she gave birth, did you know that? Before the governor had them tear it all down, had them dissolve the court of Oyer and Terminer."

"That was a blessing, however tardy," my father offered, his hand bridging over to his cousin's shoulder as he urged him to sit.

But Philip was still deep in his own thoughts, it seemed. He ignored my father and paced the room. "It took an accusation against the royal governor's own wife to do it, to dissolve that court. Why? When we returned home from our haven in New York we found our wharves, our ships, confiscated, our home an empty shell. Such was justice. It was not enough for them to have the bond that they took when we ran for our lives. No, that was not enough. We found our house ransacked by our neighbors. Every stick of furniture, gone! Our daughter's needlework, almost as perfect as her mother's. Stolen. Who would steal a child's needlework sampler lesson? Who are these people?"

He was asking unanswerable questions, so my father and I offered the only gift we had, our attention.

"We found our cow," Philip told us. "In Corwin's household. We knew her by her tail." A helpless laugh followed this revelation.

My father leaned forward. "Perhaps you should bring your family to Newfoundland. Start rebuilding your life there, with us."

The anger, so evident when we'd come to Salem, flashed again. "Give them the satisfaction of believing they were right, justified? That we were not worthy to be in the Massachusetts Bay Colony, dwelling among God's elite? His chosen? That I afflicted a maid at meeting, caused a neighbor's sons to die, his own nose to gush blood? Will that be how my family lives on in memory in their records, so meticulously written to make them the heroes of their own lives? Nay, my dear cousin! We will rebuild our fortune. We will get everything back. We will prosper. But we will never enter that meeting house again. We will never acknowledge the existence of Susannah Sheldon, and the others who accused us. And that sheriff with the heart of a beast? I will use my own two strong arms, if I must, to bring him down. To get my own back. And I will use the law that these people have such a reverence for. I will never stop my suits against him and his family." His face went from its expression of fiery rage to anguish again. "Oh, I fear I will lose her. That my love will kill my beautiful Mary, dear cousins."

"You both live," my father reminded him. "You must hope for a good birth, and Mary's heath restored."

"What was written on the gates of Dante's Inferno, Martin? 'Abandon all hope, ye who enter here?' I am afraid life has destroyed any hope left for me to abandon. I have already seen hell, thanks to my neighbors."

The next day the winds were right, so we walked Cousin Philip and his children onboard, along with Will's little farmer's blouse with the seams taken out to become a gift for the baby who would soon be welcomed with the name Ebenezer English.

Mary was the last to join them. "This life I so wished to return to, I fear it now," she confided.

I took her outstretched hand in mine. "May you be a comfort to your mother, a strength to your family."

"That will be possible only with your forgiveness, Charlotte."

I looked up at my father, his smile, his dashing face's new powder burn scar.

"You have it with all my heart," I told Mary, realizing the truth of the words as I said them.

My father, Randall and I waved from dockside, before Randall took up his bell to announce the departure of the children who had filled our rooms for the last year. My father and I lingered, reluctant to return to a house now empty of their voices.

At the end of the fall before, as Rose Brewster entered her eighth month, she was more convinced than ever that she was carrying a girl. She was also afflicted with strange cravings and desperate desires. For honeyed sweets, and briny cucumbers. And for being on the water.

Before she left our island to continue the grand tour of her holdings, Countess Amelia gifted Rose a fleet double-masted Bermuda sloop called *Edgewater*, in compensation for the loss of her husband. Rose loved the vessel. She found much joy standing on deck as my father and a few of his sailors tried out its fleet maneuvers in our waters.

She managed to convince us to take one last tour around our peninsula of Avalon before winter. A sudden storm blew us off course and into the rough waves of the open sea. My father and his crew struggled to bring us home as night was coming hard upon us.

Then Rose's laboring began.

Worry etched his face as I informed my father. "But it is not yet her time," he insisted. "She promised me it was not yet close to her time."

"The child has other ideas upon that subject, Papa."

He cupped my face in his hand. "Aye then. We shall all do our duty. Rose has you. Your mama had only me."

"And you were enough, Papa. I pray I shall be."

He kissed the worried lines from my forehead.

But without Mrs. Gavin by my side, I felt adrift. I brought to my mind the births I had attended with my grandmothers. I thought of their soft voices and steady hands. But the dark, calm recesses of a wigwam or earthen chamber was nothing like the small captain's quarters under the deck of the sloop *Edgewater*, the wind and the wave tossed tumbling of this laboring time.

Soon Rose's own waves were coming on hard and fast. Papa put his head in the door just as I was feeling my most intense loneliness without the women.

"We have sighted the harbor and are bringing her around. All is well?" he asked.

"As it should be," I made my answer, with a calmness I did not feel.

My grandmothers say you can smell this last part of the birthing time on a woman, but I had not enough experience to achieve that sense, so what I told him had an element of wishful thinking. I wanted the laboring over for my suffering friend. But in even thinking that I broke a chief admonition of their teaching. "Stay with the mother and her babe in the now, always. When a wave peaks, send it into the past, remind her she will not have to endure that one again. And as her own swells come, help her rise, float over them, meet the next." Yes. This was the great storm of the end of the rising the falling coming so close until—

"Charlotte, I must push!"

Ah. We had arrived. Together.

My father's helmsman, Mr. Janeway, was also a very fine fiddler. He donated some catgut string to tie young Master Brewster's umbilical cord before I placed him in his mother's arms. My fears of Rose rejecting her small but hearty son dissolved when I saw their eyes meet. He let out a sighing breath that was caught up and breathed in by his mother. "You've brought a change in the weather, my beautiful boy," she greeted him.

As we came into port, my father rested one arm on the sturdy side of the ship. He sheltered me in his warm embrace with the other.

"I have always said, you were good in a storm," he whispered at my ear.

The End

Afterward

It was a great joy for Jude and me to bring you *Spectral Evidence*. We hope you found it a good reading experience. Our research was endlessly fascinating. Here is some of the history behind our story.

--Eileen Charbonneau

Spectral Evidence

Could you ever imagine that a person could be sentenced to death based on spectral evidence (unseen visions)? That is what judges on both sides of the Atlantic struggled with in the seventeenth century. If someone claimed ghosts of the dead came back to accuse their murderers or a living person sent out her spirit to torment a child, it is impossible to refute their claim. And could the Devil assume an innocent person's shape?

The dilemma of the judges of Salem was: how much weight should such evidence be given? Theologians did not agree. The court judges turned to minister/scholar Cotton Mather for advice. He wrote that spectral evidence could be used if it was not the only evidence, and he urged the trials be concluded quickly to rid the Devil's influence from New England. It seems the judges listened more to the second part of his advice and by October 1692 over 200 people had been accused and 20 put to death. By the time a new court opened in 1693, the use of spectral evidence was severely limited. Acquittals began and the killings ended. Spectral evidence lost its death grip on Salem and the American colonies.

Wars of 1692

1692 was a tumultuous year in both the Old and the New Worlds. France's Louis XIV, called the Sun King had grown so powerful that a Grand Alliance (England, Spain, Savoy, Dutch Republic, and Hapsburg Monarchy) formed against France's expansionist policies. The Nine Years War (1688-1697) spanned three continents. In north America it was called King William's War. And yet, a secret alliance existed between England and France that was not discovered until a century later, leaving places like Newfoundland under protected and exposed. For the English king promised France's King Louis XIV that he would not send the English navy to the aid of his American colonists.

There was good reason for the colonists of *Spectral Evidence* to fear the French Navy. Along with the well-trained force of its army, with effectiveness increased by their friendship pacts with Native Americans like the Mi'kmaq. The French incorporated the innovative fighting methods of their allies, plus centralized leadership. But French weakness included their smaller population in the New World.

The attitude of New World colonists trying to stay out of Old World politics and conflict eventually lead to the American Revolution. The new Americans did not want to be colony without money, autonomy, self-governance, and ability to make its own finished goods.

New World attitudes against Old World conflict also led to the great and tragic displacement of neutral Acadians, who refused to fight against their French kinsman in the French and Indian War (1754-1763). They became a people scattered all over the world as refugees. Many became the Cajuns of Louisianna.

Flora and Fauna

Then as now, the island of Newfoundland is spectacular in its beauty. The rocks of the Avalon Peninsula are very old, contain ash and lava and may have once been connected to Africa. Stands of forests, open barrens and coastal headlands are home to a great many migratory birds, the mink, snowshoe hare, red fox. The Atlantic waters produced the fish that became the currency for the island, **cod**. Waters were also home to salmon, brook trout and brown trout, smelt, eel, and sticklebacks. **Puffins** did not get their current name until 1760. They were called "sea parrots" in 1692, so that is the term we used in *Spectral Evidence*. But I'm sure were just as delightful as they are today. In 1692 Newfoundland was the land of the **caribou**, which you can still see on land protected by the Avalon Wilderness Reserve. Moose were not introduced to the island until the late nineteenth century.

Bermuda and Primus's Indenture

Bermuda was tied to Newfoundland during the period of *Spectral Evidence*, as was New England. All were part of a vast trading network of British colonies. The islands were known for Bermuda cedar which were used in fleet sailing vessels. In the 17th century they were already replanting their groves if the trees so as not to deplete the islands' resources.

Black people began to immigrate to Bermuda from the West Indies as indentured servants in the mid-seventeenth century. Irish were shipped to Bermuda and sold into indentured servitude. They included Catholic civilians removed from lands that were resettled by British Protestants. The English of Bermuda feared the Irish, who plotted rebellions with Black enslaved people, and intermarried with the Black and Native American population. This fear led to terms of indenture for Black servants being raised from seven years (as with whites) to 99 years.

The Historical People in *Spectral Evidence*

Madame de Maintenon, (Francoise d'Aubigne) was Charlotte's French godmother who sent her the grey wool gown she wears in Salem. Francoise was a real person who I used for fictional purposes. She began her life among the royalty of France as the governess of Louis XIV's children. She was a gifted scholar and an innovative and compassionate teacher. Madame de Maintenon became the king's trusted counselor who spoke with him as an equal in matters economic, political, and religious. After the death of the French queen in 1683, she became Louis's second wife. The marriage was an open secret of the French court. Madame de Maintenon was never officially recognized as queen because of the vast difference between her own and Louis's social status. She indeed founded a school for the daughters of poor noble families, as is discussed in *Spectral Evidence*. It was said that the king spent some hours with his cherished second wife each day for the rest of his life. Captain Martin Jaddore, of course, calls her "our gracious queen" because he knows her secret.

Les Filles du Roi

Indentured servant Rose Brewster wistfully mentions *les Filles du Roi* when we first meet her in *Spectral Evidence*. These were not literally the daughters of King Louis XIV, but sometimes called "the King's Wards." They were a group of about 800 young women of modest means but adventurous spirits, who consented to come to New France between 1663 and 1673. Their passage and doweries were paid for by the king. Their mission: to choose husbands among the largely male population and with them start permanent settlement families. Some stayed single, some returned to France, but the program was a success. Thanks to these women, France has a population stronghold in Canada that lasts to this day. I count Filles *du Roi* among my own French Canadian ancestors, my sixth great-grandmother, Francoise Barton, and my seventh great-grandmother, Jeanne Cederet.

The English Family

Young Mary, Phillip, and William English's escape to Newfoundland was a product of my imagination. Their specific whereabouts remain unknown during their parents' exile from Salem during the height of the witch trials. But they, their parents, sister Susanna and brother Ebenezer were all real people.

The circumstances of the accusations against Philip and Mary English, their escape to Boston, then to New York are all well documented. Philip English really did send a shipment of food to the poor of Salem even during his persecution, and he feuded bitterly with his accusers, especially Sherrif Corwin. Family stories even tell of him holding his enemy's body hostage after death to receive compensation for the looting of Philip's house and fortune.

As her eldest daughter had feared in the pages of *Spectral Evidence*, Mary English did not survive long after the birth of her last child, Ebenezer.

Philip English never again congregated on Sundays with the puritan neighbors who had caused such misery for his family. He rowed his children across the Bay to Marblehead, Massachusetts to attend Church of England services. Later he funded the establishment of St. Peter's, the first Anglican church in Salem, on whose grounds he and Mary are buried.

The English sons followed their father and became merchant seamen. Daughters Mary and Susanna married sea captains. Susanna's daughter married into the Hathorne family, the same family that produced both a judge of the Salem Witch trials that convicted her grandparents, and the author of *The Scarlet Letter*, Nathanial Hawthorne

Salem remains haunted by the events of 1692-93. But it does not turn away from the story of the intolerance and injustice that plagued that troubled time. You can visit the home where Mary English was brought to be interrogated and see her exquisite needlework and an English family chair at the world-class Peabody Essex Museum. Salem has also become a place that welcomes and celebrates "witch" identified people—tarot readers, spiritual healers, shamans, neo-pagans, occultists, mystics, herbalists, folks of the gay, transgender and many formally marginalized communities.

The Beothuk

Two native people lived on Newfoundland at the time *Spectral Evidence* takes place, the Beothuk and the Mi'kmaq. The Beothuk had been keeping clear of the newcomers since the time of the Viking Settlement at L'Anse aux Meadows. They may have been the people the Vikings called Skraeling in the Norse Saga of the Greenlanders. The Beothuk began to use iron, not through trade, but by gathering up what seasonal fishermen left behind. They lived inland in winter, then camped along the shore to fish over the warmer months. As New World settlements grew, the Beothuk retreated into the interior, facing starvation. It was formally thought the nation went extinct in 1829. But the Mi'kmaq always claimed that the Beothuk live in them, as the two nations intermarried. Genetic research has proved this to be true. Beothuk DNA has also been found in the people of Iceland, so maybe those early encounters were not all unfriendly.

The Mi'kmaq

The Mi'kmaq people moved to Newfoundland after the Beothuk and lived beside them at the time of *Spectral Evidence*. They are an Algonquin language speaking Eastern Woodlands people who claim they occupied Newfoundland since pre-contact times. Their stories tell of coming over from Cape Breton. Some historians claimed that their allies the French paid them to kill Beothuk, and so they were part of the nation's extinction, but this has been disputed by the oral history of the Mi'kmaq themselves. It claims kinship and fellowship with the Beothuk, including providing havens for refugee Beothuk. Genetic research comes out on the Mi'kmaq side of this debate.

Money

Before the late 1700s, cash was rare in Newfoundland. Few English gold and silver coins circulated in any of her North American colonies. Instead, paper promissory notes facilitated trade, as they do in *Spectral Evidence*. What was this currency based on? Whatever had value, including wampum shells (Massachusetts Bay Colony until outlawed in 1660) Tobacco (Virginia), enslaved persons, and land. In

Newfoundland, the currency was dried cod, the export of the island.

The credit and barter system in English colonies helped lead indentured servants becoming farmers and craftsmen. A yeoman farmer population grew in the countryside, while craftspeople formed the basis of New World cities.

The Mummer Stag

Mummering (or "mumming") in some form can be traced from the beginnings of recorded history in the writings of the oldest peoples of Egypt, Rome, and Greece. It came to Europe in the Middle Ages and was brought to Newfoundland by the Irish and the English. What are other days when the social classes are ridiculed and turned upside down and artful disguise is in order? Mardi Gras and Halloween, of course.

St. Anne

Like Charlotte and the Mi'kmaq characters in *Spectral Evidence*, Mi'kmaq have been largely of the Catholic religion since 1610 when their chief and members of his family were baptized by Catholic missionaries. The cross was already a sacred symbol to them, representing the four directions and keeping in physical, mental, emotional, and spiritual balance. Most also did not give up their older spiritual practices when they converted. They added the ways of Christianity to them. The devotion of the

Mi'kmaq people to St. Anne is a natural outgrowth of their love and respect for the wisdom and healing ways of grandmothers. St. Anne, the grandmother of Jesus Christ was honored as a Clan Mother by people who traced their families through female lines.

Widows

Spectral Evidence features its share of widows. In a society based on travel, commerce and war by water, there were many casualties at sea, leaving many women of all classes left widows. Most quickly remarried, helping to form new households. But others, especially if they had the means, enjoyed the independence, autonomy, and greater freedoms of a widow's life too much to relinquish it.

Literacy in the Massachusetts Bay Colony

The ability to read and write was rare for all but the highest classes in the seventeenth century. An exception came by way of the Puritan Clergy, who insisted on literacy so that all could read the Bible. Therefore, Massachusetts Bay Colony had the highest literacy rate in the world. But there was a backfire... people who can read and write often can think independently. The next century was to bring the American Revolution from its birthplace: Massachusetts.

The Future Fate of St. John's

Tavernkeeper Peter Fewings's worries about what the French might do to spoil the St. John's way of life and trade were justified. As King William's War wore on, and with the secret alliance keeping any English warships from their motherland, the French raided by land and sea and burned St. John's to the ground a few years later, in 1696.

Star Trek Connection

Easter egg alert! Fans of all the versions of Star Trek might note the fun we had naming Captain Martin Jaddore's officers. We fancy them ancestors of future captains of starships.

Eileen Charbonneau is an award-winning novelist who writes for both adults and young adults. She lives in the state of Vermont but traces her heritage on her father's side to the 1659 voyage of the *St. Andre* from La Rochelle, France, to the new settlement of Montreal, Canada. Among the *St. Andre's* passengers were the first New World Charbonneaus: Oliver, Marguerite, and their three-year-old daughter Anne. Two of the sons of this family became voyagers who traded with many Native American nations of Canada and the United States. Among Eileen's distant relatives are an Ojibwe woman named Beloved Jeanne and three members of the Lewis and Clark expedition—Sacagawea of the Shoshone people, her husband Toussaint Charbonneau, and their son Jean-Baptiste.

Judith (Jude) Pittman is the author of a five book mystery series, *The Kelly McWinter PI Mysteries*. This series of novels was set in Texas, where Jude lived for several years during which time she earned her degree in Communications from Tarrant County College and became acquainted with the prototypes for the characters as well as the customs and locale that became the foundation for the *Kelly McWinter PI Mysteries*.

Jude returned to Canada in 1991, where she continued her studies at Okanagan University and continued her writing career with feature articles in the local newspaper and business profiles featuring community and university leaders. In 1992 Jude married *Metis* author *John Wisdomkeeper*.

In addition to the *Kelly McWinter PI series* Jude's published novels include *Pillars of Avalon* with Author Katherine Pym and *Mother Shipton and the Sister Witches* with Author Gail Roughton.

BWL Publishing

bwlpublishing.ca

9 780022 862949